COFFIN HOLLOW
and Other Ghost Tales

Ruth Ann Musick

COFFIN HOLLOW
and Other Ghost Tales

With a foreword by William Hugh Jansen
Illustrations by Archie L. Musick

THE UNIVERSITY PRESS OF KENTUCKY

The University Press of Kentucky
Scholarly publisher for the Commonwealth,
serving Bellarmine University, Berea College, Centre College of
Kentucky, Eastern Kentucky University, The Filson Historical Society,
Georgetown College, Kentucky Historical Society, Kentucky State
University, Morehead State University, Murray State University,
Northern Kentucky University, Transylvania University, University of
Kentucky, University of Louisville, and Western Kentucky University.
All rights reserved.

Editorial and Sales Offices: The University Press of Kentucky
663 South Limestone Street, Lexington, Kentucky 40508-4008
www.kentuckypress.com

Library of Congress Cataloging in Publication Data

Coffin Hollow, and other ghost tales / [edited by] Ruth Ann
  Musick ; with a foreword by William Hugh Jansen ; ill. by Archie
  L. Musick.—Lexington : University Press of Kentucky, © 1977.
  Bibliography: p. 193-[194]
  1. Tales, American—West Virginia. 2. Ghosts—West Virginia.
I. Musick, Ruth Ann.
GR110.W4C63   398.2'5'09754   76-51157
ISBN 0-8131-1416-0   MARC
ISBN-13: 978-0-8131-1416-3

Member of the Association of
American University Presses

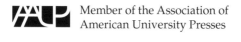

CONTENTS

A Foreword   ix

Preface   xvii

Tales   1

Notes   181

Bibliography   193

A FOREWORD

In Memoriam
RUTH ANN MUSICK
(1899-1974)

Great quantities of enthusiasm, of selfless interest in the
projects of others, of unflagging dedication to students
whose virtues she always discovered with no difficulty
whatsoever — all tightly compressed into a quite small,
feminine, intense compass: that was the late Ruth Ann
Musick, most recent in the line of fine but lonely scholars
who have personified West Virginia folklore both within
and beyond the boundaries of that state. During her
many years in the English department of Fairmont State
College, she was practically a public relations agent for
folklore within West Virginia. She made radio broadcasts;
she wrote newspaper columns; she founded, edited, and
wrote for the *West Virginia Folklore Journal*. A fine
dramatic narrator herself, she was ready at any time to
tell a West Virginia tale. The present volume is the fourth
composed of folk material collected by her in West Virginia.

She had a graduate degree in mathematics as well as
her doctorate in English (with emphasis upon creative
writing) from the State University of Iowa. With no for-
mal training in folkloristics, Dr. Musick struggled hero-
ically to make herself a professional folklorist, frequently
handicapped by limitations of time, library facilities, and
funds. When I first knew Ruth Ann Musick, she was

assiduously taking notes and attending every session from early morning to late night in Dr. Stith Thompson's summer Folklore Institute at Indiana University. No one could have more appreciated the opportunities afforded by the splendid library or the chance to study with famous authorities gathered from all over the world.

She was an early disciple of Vance Randolph. It would be difficult to find a more scholarly or a more unlikely mentor. Until her death she remained a concerned and loyal follower. One of her last letters expressed deep worry that some song manuscripts entrusted to her long ago by Randolph might now go unpublished.

Somehow peculiarly typical of her is her last correspondence with this memorialist. With no ostentation, no self-pity, she cited the grim probabilities about her impending death as reason for despair about finishing her projects. Her concern was for her student informants and collectors whose materials might never be seen and for her respected folklorist peers who might not therefore fully appreciate the wealth of folklore that distinguished her adopted state. With an embarrassing modesty that I once erroneously took for irony, she sought approval (granted, of course!) of a plan to present her manuscripts to Fairmont State College, trusting that there they would be available to all scholars.

In what is likely to be a more productive plan, Dr. Musick finally charged two dedicated literary executrixes with the responsibility of administering her unpublished folklore materials. Judy Prozzillo Byers and Catherine Faris not only intend to prepare various manuscripts for publication but also are encouraging the establishment of a folklore archive (with the Musick manuscripts) and a folklore institute at Fairmont State College — all proposed as a continuation of Ruth Ann Musick's efforts. In the last twenty years of her life, Dr. Musick, whose early interest in folklore had been predominantly in ballad and folk song, concentrated more and more upon the legend, upon the narrative performed in the belief that it is literally or, occasionally, figuratively true. In *Folktales Told around the World* (Chicago: University of Chicago Press, 1975), his latest and greatest work, Dr. Richard M. Dorson points out that *legend* should be understood as one genre of *folktale*, that scholarly neglect alone has caused *legend* and *folktale* to be considered somehow mutually exclusive terms. He notes that although the Grimms' *Märchen* (fairy tales) have innumerable English translations, their *Sagen* (legends) have not even once been published in English. Dr. Dorson attributes the neglect to the fact that legends are too allusive, too unstructured, too fragmentary (p. xx).

However, as Dr. Dorson also indicates, legends have recently begun to receive scholarly attention. Although the Baughman *Type and Motif Index of the Folktales of England and North America* is an invaluable aid (witness Dr. Musick's notes in this volume) to establishing the traditional quality of specific legends, it has clear self-imposed linguistic and geographic limitations. And it will be a long time before a majority of the legends of England and, particularly, North America are published and available for type- and motif-indexing. Although ten of Dr. Musick's articles are in the Baughman *Index*, naturally neither this volume nor her *Telltale Lilac Bush* of 1965 is so indexed. Someday inevitably there will be a supplement to Baughman or a separate legend index, and it will draw upon the Musick volumes.

Legends, of course, are not restricted to the oral tradition, a fact that zealous folklorists sometimes forget. Historians have recorded legends; journalists have committed legends; professional writers, serious and comic, skilled and inept, have created some legends and recorded others. Most — all, we hopefully assume — legends have spent a major part of their existence in the oral tradition. Most are born in the oral tradition, and some of these move into a literary tradition. Others, born in the literary tradition, move easily into the oral tradition. And for a single legend the transition may happen over and over. Who could trace the migrations of "The Vanishing Hitchhiker" through a cinema version, a television show, a country western song, several journalistic articles, and dozens of straight-faced "news" accounts, particularly when each "nontraditional" appearance may be sandwiched into the midst of authentic orally performed "traditional" appearances?

Coffin Hollow stands in the middle of the traditional-nontraditional, literary-oral debate. With candor that it would be foolish to mistake for naïveté — it is really quite wittingly defiant — Dr. Musick points out in her preface that despite her four tape machines, 90 percent or more of the legends here were presented to her in writing by her students. She maintains vehemently and quite correctly that these legends are from oral tradition, and in general her documentation and citation of motifs bear out her contention.

The oral tradition has an aural aspect, an aspect that appeals to, and is recognized by, experienced listeners to oral performance. It is an aspect created in the performance by the listener, and it gives to oral narrative performance part of its aesthetic value. One effect of the aural aspect is that the experienced folk listener is not bothered by, does not even notice, the allusive unstructured, fragmentary shortcomings cited above by Dr. Dorson as reasons for the scholars' disaffection for the legend.

It is this aural aspect that Dr. Musick's students ignored as they represented in writing for experienced readers (not for experienced listeners) narratives in the oral tradition. It can be cogently argued that any other procedure would be impossible, but that argument belongs elsewhere. The procedure used here presents readable (by readers' standards) legends, legends that have been given narrative form by recorders who were writing down tales they knew but to which they themselves applied literary rather than folk standards. The allusions (i.e., the substitution or insertion of local family and geographical names into tales told about other families and other places, a process committed not by the present recorder but by some skilled narrator in the perhaps remote past) make independent tales out of versions of one type. The structural patterns lead to climaxes and to closing statements that create a sense of completion.

Indeed there are stories here that are too polished. Oral narrators love the trick of withholding an important detail from their audiences until the very end of the performance, where it suddenly enlightens or shocks. This device is used too adroitly in a few tales — e.g., 85, 86, 87 (where the punch is withheld until the last three words), 92, and 95. But polished or no, the core is from the oral tradition and each narrative is a recognizable legend.

There are other and more important points that distinguish the *Coffin Hollow* collection as legendary and as oral tradition. It has the hitchhiking ghosts that one

xiii

expects of any collection, the headless trainmen, the murdered pack peddlers, the ineradicable bloodstains that go with any Appalachian collection, and the bitter Civil War legends common to the Border States. Very exciting is the proliferation of a single tale type; there are eleven quite independent forms of "The Vanishing Hitchhiker" (Baughman number E332.3.3.1), one of which (50) is not so identified by the arrangement. There are two full versions and one partial version of conventional Tale Type 326, all beautifully localized and convincingly "true" or allusive: 22, 44, and 81 (in part). Tale 51 is really built around E544: Ghost leaves evidence of his appearance, a motif made famous fifty years ago by Alexander Woollcott and known long before that. There is even a shaggy dog story (45).

Of the many fascinating motifs let me mention but two: the magic properties acquired by an apple tree on which a man has been unjustly hanged (35 and 56) and the headless dog that steals rides behind a man on horseback (47). I suspect a continental European source for the apple tree, but I have no guess about the origin of the headless dog of Tug Fork (though it obviously builds on E332.3.1).

Folk speech here (not dialect: see Dr. Musick's preface) also excitingly comments on the oral tradition. In an area that knows pickup trucks, sedans, coupes, and hardtops, a buggy is made implausibly capacious (36), but at the same time in a state where coal mining is a major occupation, *slack* is used correctly in a very peculiar British miners' definition (37). I also would propose that the place name *Darkish Knob* (27) represents a misunderstanding on the part of recorder and informant of a place name legend for *Darkies' Knob*.

There are many other points to be made. The appearance here of narrative infelicities that would go unnoticed in the aural-oral context again bespeaks the origin of the material. And some very successful tales are in the collection — e.g., 13 and the emotional 55, with its beautiful use of the motif of the unquiet spirit.

I suppose and hope that other volumes will be quarried from Dr. Musick's literary estate. Nothing could better serve her crusade for the recognition of West Virginia folklore.

WILLIAM HUGH JANSEN
University of Kentucky

PREFACE

West Virginia is truly a beautiful state, although its beauty may very well be doomed. The strip miners seem so determined to scalp the hills and slice off the topsoil — to get at the little bit of coal that lies near the surface — that they are fast skinning the state alive. Also lumbermen — clear-cutters — continue to mow down the trees, and so-called sportsmen are slaughtering much of the wildlife. West Virginia may soon become just an ordinary state — well, *worse* than ordinary — a completely sodless, treeless, creatureless land, unless it can be saved.

For years now I've been trying to save just the stories and general lore of West Virginia. To me, these tales are almost as fascinating and individual as the state itself. One of the things I particularly like is that the tale-tellers are so sincere. Aside from legends — and no one knows exactly how a legend originates — these tales are told as the actual experiences of the contributors or of their relatives or friends. In almost every case the original teller, at least, believes that he or the person involved has had a supernatural experience.

While most outsiders seem to think that all — or almost all — West Virginians speak some kind of colorful, unsoiled-by-schooling, mountain dialect, something like the language of Little Abner and the Dogpatch clan, I have not found much of this speech used by the storytellers I have met. Undoubtedly there are isolated sections in the state where Anglo-Saxon or peculiarly mountain expressions are common; but I have heard almost nothing of such dialect, much as I would like to, and I've lived in the state for years. Furthermore, the people who have shared their lore with me have evidently never heard much, if any, of this speech either.

Although I have used every method known to man in collecting folklore — I have bought four tape machines, to date — I am indebted to former students at Fairmont State College for much of my material, especially the stories. I would say that some 90 percent or more of all my ghost tales were brought in by my students, who got them from their parents, grandparents, or older neighbors in most cases. Although some tales were told orally, a great deal of this material was written up when it was brought in, and besides deleting extraneous material or transferring it to the notes, I have kept the tales as they were given to me, merely correcting student errors of grammar and spelling — faults one can hardly blame on the original contributor or call authentic folklore.

Vance Randolph collected all his material from the Ozark people themselves, so that his dialect is both colorful and authentic, as it should be. So far, I can't follow his example, much as I would like to do so, for I have heard almost no dialect here. However, I would like to point out that I have been able to collect hundreds and hundreds of ghost tales — most of which I would have had no way in the world to get except through my students. Older people may very well object to telling any supernatural experiences to outsiders, but they usually have no objections whatever to telling such happenings to younger relatives or neighbor youngsters whom they have watched grow up.

Some of the tales in this collection were previously published in *North Carolina Folklore, West Virginia Folklore,* the *Charleston Gazette-Mail State Magazine*, the *Morgantown Dominion-Post Panorama*, and the *Allegheny Journal*. I wish to thank the editors involved for permission to use this material again.

Also I wish to thank all the contributors of stories, since without their help there could have been no book. I particularly want to thank my former students at Fairmont State College, especially those who became so interested in my love of lore that they combed their communities in order to get together as much material as possible. My enthusiasm for ghost tales must have been fairly obvious from the start, since so many of them were brought in. I also want to thank the relatives and neighbors involved, who gave so generously of their time.

Last of all, I want to express my appreciation of my brother's illustrations, which add so much in helping to portray the supernatural situations as told in the tales.

RAM
Fairmont, September 1973

TALES

1: A Strange Illusion

It was a cold night. And with the chilly air came lightning and thunder. Soon the rain began to come down in torrents. No one was out except for one man — a young traveler who, because his horse had gone lame, was forced to go on by foot.

Of course he had to seek shelter some place, and that is why he stopped at the first house he came to — a large old mansion. His knock went unanswered, so he called out, "Is anybody home?"

There was no response. Lightning and thunder echoed over the hills, and the weary traveler turned the door knob. To his amazement he found the door unlocked. It shrieked and creaked on its hinges when he pushed it open. Probably the old mansion was deserted, yet strangely enough the rooms seemed to be furnished.

The traveler shut the door and went to a chair. Folding his damp coat under his head, he prepared to go to sleep. He had begun to doze when suddenly the old grandfather clock started to strike twelve. Down the winding staircase came a young girl carrying a lantern. The youth jumped to his feet and said, "The ——— door was loose and open, so I walked in out of the rain."

The girl just smiled and vanished into another room. Soon she came back carrying a tray of food and steaming hot coffee. She gestured for him to eat and then extended one of the cups to him. The girl did not make one sound. Instead a mysterious smile played about her lips. Never had the traveler tasted such fine food. When the meal was over, the girl gathered up the tray and went back to the kitchen.

3

After a while, when she did not return, the man began to smell what he thought was wood smoke. Afraid that something might have caught on fire in the kitchen, he ran into the adjoining room. There was no girl there, and things seemed to be in order. Thinking that there was another way out of the kitchen and the girl had probably taken it, the sleepy youth wandered back into the next room and sank into the chair. Not another thought came to his mind, and soon he was asleep.

Before he knew it, morning came. Birds twittered outside the window. A tray of fresh food was before him. When he looked up, there stood the smiling girl. Probably she was a deaf-mute, he thought, as she never spoke. The traveler thanked her for the food and shelter, finished eating, and said good day to the girl, telling her to look him up if she ever needed a favor.

As he entered the outskirts of the town, he was met by a mob, who led him off to the sheriff's office. It seemed that an old man had been beaten very seriously during the night. Everyone in town was pointing an accusing finger at any stranger who arrived. So far all suspects were able to justify their whereabouts. Could the Traveler?

Once inside the sheriff's office, he was asked where he had been during the night. When he explained about being at the mansion and how grateful he was for the warm hospitality extended him, a few of the men laughed, but some of the elderly men frowned and walked away.

"I gotta lock you up, boy," said the sheriff. "That's one story that just can't stand true. The old Cathcart mansion was the only one near here, and it burned down five years ago." There was nothing to do except to lock the traveler up in jail.

After the morning hours dragged into midafternoon and the earlier confusion had died down, the young traveler had time to think. "Sheriff, why don't you and I drive out there and take a look at the place where I stayed? Maybe it can prove my innocence."

Being kind and considerate, the sheriff agreed. After all, the man did not have a guilty look, and if he had any way of proving his innocence, the sheriff was going to let him try.

Hitching up a horse and buggy, the two men started toward the outskirts of town. Before one comes to the Cathcart estate, a turn in the road obstructs the house from view. As they drew near this turn the young man said confidently, "You'll see, sheriff, that place is where I stayed." But instead of a big white mansion, there was only a red brick chimney staring upward, with charred ashes on the ground.

The sheriff put a comforting hand on the shocked traveler's shoulder. "I'm sorry, boy, but now you can see for yourself. That place burned five years ago. Old man Cathcart's daughter, who people claimed was mentally ill because she always smiled, was burned to death. Hamilton Cathcart tried to save her and was badly burned. He died later at the hospital."

The traveler hung his head sadly as the carriage headed back to town. The only witness in the world who could save his life — and she wasn't there! Who was the woman he had seen then? There were no other houses around. This definitely was the place where he had stayed during the night. Could it be that he had seen a ghost?

The sheriff was talking. "Yes, sir, it was rumored that old man Cathcart was carrying on a feud with Charlie Pickens over some love affair between Melissa Cathcart and young Charlie Pickens, Jr. Some folks think Pickens set the place on fire, hoping to destroy Cathcart and his young daughter. There was no evidence against him, so he went free. Before old Cathcart died, his last words were, 'I'll get even with the one who did this to me! He'll pay!' People didn't pay much attention to him, as they figured he was out of his head."

The sheriff lit a pipe and drew a long breath. The young traveler asked, "What happened to old man Pickens?"

"That's why we're holding you," the sheriff answered. "Old man Pickens was the guy that got beat up. If he dies, you'll be tried for murder. Right now you can't prove your innocence, and we can't prove your guilt. But if he dies we'll have you on circumstantial evidence."

At this the traveler's heart sank. He asked, "Sheriff, why don't we go to the hospital and see old man Pickens? He might help my case."

The sheriff agreed. "If old man Pickens is conscious, we may get a few questions cleared up. I'd still like to know for myself if he did set the Cathcart place on fire."

The rest of the trip was made in silence. Inside the old two-story hospital, a few members of the Pickens family hurried to the door as the sheriff entered. "He's been calling for you, sheriff," they said.

The sheriff leaned over to hear the faint whispers coming from the dying man. "The traveler is innocent . . . I burned the Cathcart place and now . . . old Cathcart is just getting even with me."

At that instant, a huge cloud of black smoke came out with Pickens's breath. For a split second flames and smoke engulfed his body. They were gone as quickly as they came and left the body burned beyond recognition.

From out of nowhere a man's voice was heard saying, "I got even with you!" The words were followed by a harsh laugh.

The case was closed then, and the traveler went on his way — a free man. But never again did he venture into this strange town.

2: The Jailer's Dog

Many years ago in the town of Brownsville, Pennsylvania, there was a small jail run by a very friendly and just sheriff. Sheriff Davis and his big dog were usually the sole occupants of the jail, but on one particular night a boy was brought in who had got drunk and destroyed property at one of the local bars.

Sheriff Davis locked him up in a cell and proceeded to doze off in his bed. His faithful dog Rusty lay at his feet, as usual.

In the middle of the night the sheriff was awakened by the barking of his dog. He jumped to his feet and saw the darting figure of the boy dashing out of the door of the jail. Without thinking, he grabbed his gun and fired over the boy's head. The bullet was defective, as often was the case in those days, and, instead of following a true course, it dropped, hitting the boy in the base of the skull and killing him instantly.

Sheriff Davis was never the same after that. Although still running a very good jail, he was no longer kindly toward fellow humans or to his old dog Rusty, whom he had loved so dearly. Now, the big dog no longer slept at his feet, but spent the cold nights tied to a pole in the back of the jail. Davis was also known to take his problems out on Rusty by kicking and mistreating him. The dog had grown unfriendly toward his master, who no longer fed him. The neighbors, with whom Rusty was still friendly, now provided his food, but whenever Davis appeared, the dog immediately flew into a mad fit of rage, snarling and snapping viciously until the man beat him into quietness.

One day Rusty gnawed through his rope and ran away to one of the houses nearby, only to be dragged home by Davis, who again proceeded to beat him into submission. This time Rusty no longer stirred. The next day he was buried by the neighborhood children, who loved him and gave him the only kindness he knew.

Davis grew worse and turned to bottle-drinking — to excess. He lost his job as sheriff and stayed around the jail only to keep the place clean. He was thought to be crazy, for often in his drunken rage, he would yell, scream, threaten, and plead for Rusty to stop following him and haunting him. He often heard snarling and footsteps behind him, although nothing could be observed by anyone else.

One night when he was drunker than usual, he flew past the startled new sheriff and out the door, yelling at a nonexistent foe.

He was found the next day lying beside the post to which Rusty used to be tied, with his throat completely ripped out. About the ground were the footprints of a large dog.

The sheriff had heard the howling of a dog or wolf the preceding night, but had thought little about it. No dogs or wolves were ever found in the area. Wolves were seldom seen, and there were no dogs — that is, dogs large enough to do the damage which had been done — except Rusty.

3: Coffin Hollow

On a point of land just below my home is a very old cemetery. This cemetery contains the graves of some Civil War soldiers who died during the Jones's raid. It is said that one of these soldiers was killed after being captured by the Yanks. This gallant Confederate soldier fought long and hard before being shot in the leg by some unidentified traitor. He was then taken prisoner, loaded on a wagon, and started on his way to prison.

Now a certain Yankee captain had seen his brother shot down by this soldier and hated him for it. He set out in pursuit of the wagon, caught up with it, and like the lowly Yankee dog that he was, placed a bullet through the rebel's head, killing him instantly. The reb was buried in the cemetery previously mentioned and was forgotten.

Some years later, however, the Yankee captain moved to Monongah and began courting a girl from Watson. To get to this girl's house, he had to ride past the cemetery where the soldier was buried. On the first night that he passed the grave, he heard a loud rumble and then that blood-curdling rebel yell. Looking up toward the cemetery, he saw the soldier he had killed, seated atop his coffin, riding it over the hill toward him.

The ex-captain gave a scream, wheeled his horse around, and ran for home. The ghost followed him only as far as the mouth of the hollow, there turning back to his grave. This went on for months on end, until one night some of the captain's friends found him shot through the head with an apparently very old and previously used bullet.

Now these men had heard the captain's story and also knew that the bullet had never been removed from the dead rebel's head. They quickly went to the graveyard and opened the dead man's grave. They found there, to their horror, that the bullet was gone from the reb's head and in his hand was a still-smoking revolver.

From that time on, the wild rebel scream has never again echoed through the hollow, nor has the dead soldier ridden his coffin over the hill. However, to this day, the hollow where this took place is still called Coffin Hollow, and I can still show you the grave of the dead rebel.

4: Earl Booth's Pot of Gold

In the late 1880s Earl Booth was considered a wealthy man. He owned a large farm in Barbour County on which he raised cattle and operated a saw mill. He was also known for his unusual trading ability.

Through his enterprises he accumulated a small fortune, but instead of putting his money in the local bank, he buried it at several locations on his farm. It was well known in the community that Booth did not trust banks and would not deposit any of his earnings with them.

Two strangers were traveling through the community, and when they stopped at the general store for supplies, they overheard a conversation about Booth's hidden money. After leaving the store, they made plans to go to the farm and torture the man until he told them where his fortune was buried. They waited until he was asleep and, after entering through a window on the opposite side of the house, slipped into his bedroom and awakened him.

When they threatened his life, he told them where some of his money was buried, and while one man watched him, the other found a shovel and went to look for the treasure. After digging a shallow hole, he uncovered a small chest of silver and gold coins.

When the man returned to the house, the two talked the matter over and decided they had been tricked. Booth refused to tell where the larger portion of his fortune was buried, and the two beat him to death. But before dying, he placed a curse on the two men and said that he would return as a ghost to protect his fortune.

Fearing they would be caught, the two left the community, planning to return and find the rest of the money. Three years later they came back to the Booth farm during the night and set up a camp in the forest near the farmhouse.

The next day they started to look for the rest of the fortune. While digging under a large rock, one of the men was killed when the weight of the rock shifted and crushed him to death. The other one, thinking Booth's curse was to blame, attempted to escape. However, as he was riding away, a neighbor recognized him as one of the strangers who had passed through the community on the day of the murder.

After some questioning, he admitted helping beat Booth to death. Although he had confessed the murder, he never stood trial. Two days later he was found dead in his cell. Apparently he had died of heart failure. He looked as though he had been frightened to death during the night.

No one has ever been able to locate Earl Booth's fortune. Some people believe Booth's ghost is still guarding the gold which will remain buried forever on his old farm.

5: Revenge of an Oil Worker

In the early 1900s, the oil fields around Smithfield were booming and men of all types gathered there to work at the oil wells.

While pitching hay one day, the son of a farmer fell on his pitchfork and was killed. A worker from one of the oil derricks came upon the boy, pulled the pitchfork out of his chest, and was standing over him with the pitchfork in his hand when four men came along and saw him.

Not knowing what had happened, they accused the oil worker of murdering the boy. They had had a few drinks, and since they were a hot-headed group and good friends of the boy's father, they decided to take justice into their own hands. One of the men got a rope and threw it over the limb of a nearby tree while the others dragged the protesting, innocent oil worker over to the tree. They slipped the noose over the man's head and around his neck, and asked him if there were any last words he wished to speak.

He spit in their faces and said that he would see to it that they would all die in the same way he did within thirteen days. They then hurriedly finished the hanging and decided that one of them would take the body and bury it. Jones was the unlucky one, and when the others left he loaded the body onto a wagon and started for the woods.

Along this road was a steep embankment about twenty feet high. Somehow Jones's horse turned the wagon over, flipping Jones out and down over the hill, where his neck was caught by two branches of a tree, and he was killed. When his body was found, there wasn't much thought of the incident – nor was the body of the oil worker found.

Three days afterward, a second of the four men was found hanging from the hay mow of his barn where he had seemingly tripped on a clean floor and had fallen onto a rope he had used to haul things up into the loft.

The other two men were getting jittery and began to suspect that the oil worker's prediction was coming true – and to wonder who would be the next. They didn't have to wait long to find out because the third man was found hanging by the neck between two of the steel crosspieces of an oil derrick nine days after the last accident. The next night, which if you have counted correctly makes thirteen days from the hanging of the oil worker, the last of the four men was found hanging from a rafter in his kitchen, where he had committed suicide. for an unknown reason.

It may have been coincidence, but all four men died, just as the innocent oil worker said they would.

6: The Shue Mystery

Edward S. Shue was convicted in the Greenbrier County Circuit Court at Lewisburg, West Virginia, in June 1897, for the slaying of his young wife. The evidence was entirely circumstantial and was dreamed by Mrs. Shue's elderly mother, who was sleeping in her home fourteen miles away from the scene of the killing, on the other side of Sewell Mountain.

In four separate dreams Mrs. Heaster's daughter rose from the grave and described how her husband had murdered her. The aged woman set about trying to get enough people to believe her story so that her daughter's husband could be brought to justice. But people laughed at her at first because Mrs. Shue had been examined by a reputable doctor who pronounced her dead of natural causes. However, Mrs. Heaster was so insistent about her daughter's visits that she soon had a number of believers in her cause.

Neighbors of the late Mrs. Shue heard the strange story and began to recall some very unusual incidents that had occurred just after the young woman had been found dead. Although they had seemed of no importance at the time, these incidents raised suspicions against Shue, the village blacksmith. He had never left the head of his wife's coffin while friends and relatives were paying their last respects. When the doctor rushed to her house, he had found Shue holding his wife's body tenderly in his arms. During the doctor's examination Shue did not once let go of her head as he cried and prayed for her to come back to life. But she was beyond help.

15

Shue had married pretty Miss Zona Heaster in November 1896 at the Methodist Church at Livesay's Mill. After their marriage they lived in a small two-story frame building that had been the residence of the late William G. Livesay, who had given the settlement its name. Shue, a towering man of unknown strength, had come to Greenbrier County a short time before to work for James Crookshanks at his blacksmith shop. Miss Heaster had married him despite the fact that he had had two previous wives, both of whom had died suddenly.

The young bride became quite ill in January 1897 and for several weeks was under the care of Dr. J. M. Knapp. Shue seemed to be very concerned. On the morning of January 22, he appeared at the cabin of "Aunt" Martha Jones, mother of Anderson Jones, a Negro lad of eleven years who later became, and possibly still is, a respected resident of Lewisburg. Shue asked if the boy could go to his house and do some chores for Mrs. Shue. His mother said he still had work to do for Dr. Knapp. Shue finally made him promise to do the chores later in the day and came back four times to see if the boy could go.

About one o'clock Jones set out for the house. Nobody answered his knock, so he entered the kitchen. When he didn't see Mrs. Shue, he opened the dining room door and stumbled over her body. He raced to the blacksmith shop to tell Shue, who ran to the house while the boy went on to get Dr. Knapp. When the doctor reached the house, Shue had placed his wife on her bed and was holding her head in his arms, crying for her to come back. But strangest of all, although no one thought of it at the time, was the fact that he had placed an old-fashioned high, stiff collar around her neck and was holding it in place with some kind of scarf. Dr. Knapp immediately

16

started investigating to see if she were still alive. All the time he was trying to revive the woman, Shue refused to let him examine her head.

The next morning Mrs. Shue's body was taken over the mountain to Mrs. Heaster's home and was buried in the family graveyard on Monday. Shue never once left his dead wife's side when others were around. He placed a folded sheet on one side of his wife's head, and some garment on the other side to keep it in an upright position.

Several days after the funeral Mrs. Heaster was awakened by a noise in her cabin home. She had been praying constantly since her daughter's death to find the real cause. As she looked around in the darkened room she saw her daughter standing there in the very dress she had died in. As her mother reached out to touch her, she disappeared. The next night the girl reappeared and talked freely to her mother.

It took four visits for the murdered woman to relate the entire story to her mother. Mrs. Heaster then enlisted the help of Prosecuting Attorney John A. Preston, who firmly believed the woman after talking with her. He began his investigation by questioning Dr. Knapp, who admitted that his verdict of heart failure could be wrong. They agreed that an autopsy would prove whether Mrs. Heaster's theory was right or wrong.

The next day Dr. Knapp and Preston went to Livesay's Mill and ordered Shue to accompany them to the grave. Preston ordered several neighbors to open the grave and had to threaten arrest before they would do it, because such a thing had never been heard of in Greenbrier County. Dr. Knapp worked for three days and nights before he found what Mrs. Heaster had predicted.

Mrs. Shue's body was returned to the grave, and Shue was arrested for first-degree murder by Sheriff Bill Nickell and was placed in jail without bond to wait for the June term of court under Judge J. M. McWhorter. Preston and his assistant, Henry Gilmer, spent the intervening months collecting further evidence. Shue had asked Dr. William Rucker and James P. D. Gardner to defend him. Gardner was the first black attorney to practice in the Greenbrier Court. The case finally came before the court on June 30, 1897.

At the trial Dr. Knapp said Mrs. Shue's death was neither accidental nor a suicide. Anderson Jones told of finding the body, and others said Shue had been the only person seen at his house that morning. Still others told how he had dressed her with the stiff collar, a large veil, several times folded, and a large bow under the chin. It was also said that he hadn't acted like a normal husband who had just lost his bride of only a few months. Mrs. Heaster's evidence proved so interesting that Thomas H. Dennis, the editor of the *Greenbrier Independent* at Lewisburg, printed her entire testimony, something practically unheard of in the daily newspapers of that day.

Mrs. Heaster related to the jury the reason her daughter had given for Shue's action. He had become so angry because his wife had no meat cooked for supper that he had squeezed her neck off at the first joint.

The elderly woman was convinced that her daughter had come back to her in flesh and blood and not as a ghost. She was in the dress she had been killed in, and as she was leaving from one of her visits, she turned her head completely around to prove that her neck was disjointed. Mrs. Heaster said that these four visits were not dreams, that she was not superstitious, and that she

18

believed in the Scriptures. She also said that she had touched the girl to see if people came back from their coffins. The girl was flesh and blood, although cold to the touch.

7: The Peddler's Story

The house appeared to me to be just an old place that nobody thought good enough to live in, though it seemed sturdy and sound. I wondered why nobody was living in it since there weren't enough houses in the area.

My mother told me about the only family that had ever lived there. She couldn't remember their names, but they had come to this particular farm as one of the earliest families and settled near what is now the town of Harman, West Virginia. The man and his boys were very rough in their language and in their actions, but they knew a great deal about farming and the construction of buildings. They had built this house. It was one of the first buildings in the neighborhood.

The whole family seemed to have a mean disposition. They would lie, cheat, or steal if it meant any kind of personal gain. Their unfortunate neighbors would shake their heads and say, "They will not get away with all of this. They will get their punishment. Just you wait and see."

One evening a peddler stopped at their house and asked to spend the night. They agreed only after he had offered to pay them well. During the night the father crept into the peddler's bedroom and killed him. He

19

removed several hundred dollars from his wallet too. He then went back to bed, planning to bury the peddler in the morning.

With the coming of daylight some visiting neighbors arrived. The women of the household kept the visitors outside while the man tried to find a place to dump the dead body. There were some loose boards in the kitchen floor; the man tore them up and he and his sons buried the peddler there. When the visitors finally came into the kitchen they found the men repairing the floor "in order to keep the house in good condition." This should have been the end of the story but the peddler's death would not go unavenged.

Almost every night after the murder, the ghost of the victim roamed the house. It kept tearing at the boards, trying to get to its body, and visited the murderer several times each night. The man was so frightened that he could neither sleep nor eat. Yet he did not take his family and move away. There seemed to be some strange power forcing him to stay in that house.

One night, when he could stand the visits of the ghost no longer, he fled from the house screaming and has never been heard of since. His family ran to a neighbor's house and told their story in hopes that the ghost wouldn't visit them there. They returned to the house the next day, gathered all their possessions together, and nobody has ever heard of them since that time.

I can't say whether the house is haunted or not, but nobody has lived in it since its first occupants. The old folks of this area stay far away from the place because they say they can still hear the ghost of the peddler at night, tearing at the boards of the kitchen floor and trying to get to its body.

8: The Black Dog Ghost

During the American Revolution, near Connellsville, Pennsylvania, a spy and his dog were captured by the British and taken back to headquarters to stand trial. That very night the spy was sentenced to death and was taken out in the yard to be shot. When he was outside, he tried to escape and was cut to shreds by a soldier with a sword. When the dog saw this, it leaped at the swordsman with a fierce growl, but the soldier turned in time to stab the large black hound with his sword. As the dog lay on the ground dying, it stared at the soldier with a fierce look of hate. The soldier laughed and gave the dog a hard kick in the side to finish it off.

That night, while another soldier was coming back from guard duty, he noticed a large black hound lying near the campfire, just like the one his comrade had killed. When he walked over to the dog, it disappeared before his eyes. The soldier went to tell the man who killed the dog what had happened and to warn him that he should be careful, since he would be on duty that night. The soldier took it as a joke. He told his comrades the story and made fun of his friend who had warned him.

That night when the soldier went out on guard duty, a mysterious thing happened. The rest of the men were awakened by the fierce growls of a dog and the screams of their comrade out on guard duty. Terrified by these horrible screams of agony, they gathered around the campfire. Finally the screams halted, and something was heard crashing through the bushes.

After a few minutes the soldier who had been on guard duty came into the light of the campfire with his clothes torn to shreds, but not a scratch on his body. When the men asked him what had happened, he could not speak a word, but just stared off into the darkness of the night. Finally, on the third night, the soldier died from fright. The very minute of his death the cries of the dog ceased and were heard no more.

9: The Barn Ghost

Many, many years ago an old farmer was preparing to start to town to buy his supplies for the month. It was not unusual for farmers to go to town once a month to buy supplies for themselves and their families. This day, however, was to be unusual. The farmer, whom we shall call Jed Smith although his first name is not definitely known, was to have a strange experience.

Jed left home at about seven o'clock that morning in order to get into town before the stores opened. It was about five miles and would take every bit of the time to travel the old rugged road with his large wagon. After he had hitched up the horses and had gotten the lunch his wife had fixed for him to eat in town, he started on his day's journey. This is the last clear account we have of old Jed Smith.

When Jed didn't return by dark, his wife was naturally worried. She couldn't imagine what had happened to him. The closest neighbors lived three miles away, and

Mrs. Smith decided not to try to walk to their house and ask if they had seen Jed, because their house wasn't even close to the road.

The next morning, when Jed still hadn't returned, Mrs. Smith set out to find him. She finally learned that he and his team had fallen off the road and down a high cliff and had all been killed. She found it hard to believe that it was an accident, because her husband was a good driver and knew the road well. Maybe someone had forced him off the road on purpose.

One day Mrs. Smith went to the barn and was startled to see her husband's ghost. It must have been a ghost, because it told her that his murderer would be punished in the same way he had died. Then the image was gone.

A few months later a stranger called at Mrs. Smith's home and tried to buy her property. He said he had heard of her husband's accident and knew it would be hard for her to keep up the farm. There was something in his voice which made him sound very anxious to obtain the place, but when Mrs. Smith refused, he left in a hurry.

A few days later Mrs. Smith heard some more news. A neighbor stopped at her house and told her that a stranger had been killed at the very spot where her husband had died. The neighbor went on to say that he was an oil dealer and would do anything to get land he thought might have oil on it.

That night Mrs. Smith put the whole story together. She now remembered her husband had told her that the last time he had gone to town a man had wanted to buy their land. He had told her that when he refused to sell it the man had said that he would get it one way or another. Her husband had remarked to her then that he would rather die than sell the land.

23

Mrs. Smith wept quietly as she thought of her husband's strong will and also of his death.

10: The Miner's Wife

One night a miner became ill and left work early to go home. When he arrived, he walked straight to the bedroom to arouse his wife to fix something for his illness. As he entered the room he found his wife there with another man.

The enraged miner grabbed the man and gave him a thorough beating. After throwing him out of the house, he returned to his wife for an explanation. An argument followed and the wife, laughing at him, said she wanted a divorce. Shame mounted upon shame, and the miner returned to work, forgetting his illness.

When he got back, he told his friends what had happened and swore revenge. Still angry, he began working carelessly. An hour or so later, when a coal car was coming down the tracks, the miner fainted and fell in front of it. The other men did not notice until it was too late, and the car ran over him, crushing his head and legs.

At the funeral the miners remembered that the dead man had said that, if anything ever happened to him, he would return to get revenge upon his wife. The men told his widow, but she just laughed, saying that she was going to marry her lover and move far away from there. As it turned out, the man she was cheating with left town after the accident. She was now left by herself. Heartbroken and very lonely, she was seen only when she went out to buy groceries.

Then, one dark and dreary night, exactly one year after the accident, a terrible thing happened. It was a little after twelve o'clock when her neighbors heard a scream from the widow's house. They quickly gathered outside the house and called, but no answer was heard. The men decided to break down the door to find out what had happened.

When they got to the bedroom the door was locked, and they broke it down to see what was wrong. The widow's body was lying across the bed, the face scratched beyond recognition.

What caused this no one is really sure. Could it really have been her husband, who had come back for the revenge he swore that he would take?

11: Yankee Thrift

My grandfather, who was an engineer and demanded reason and fact for everything that happened, often made the statement that those who believed in ghosts were fools. When he spoke of the old house on Eighth Avenue in Huntington, West Virginia, however, his attitude changed.

Soon after he returned from the Spanish-American War, he learned of a beautiful, two-story house that was for sale at a very low price — so low, in fact, that he thought the price had been misquoted. Since he was a

thrifty Yankee, he was afraid of missing the opportunity of a lifetime; therefore, he rushed to make the purchase. Upon closing the sale, he was told that the previous owner had been unable to keep a renter for the property; for some reason no one would live in the house for more than one night at a time. Renters would usually leave before morning and send a teamster in to move their furniture the next day. Grandfather decided that after the family was settled in their new home he would pay a visit to one of the former occupants. This is the story that was related to him.

A very wealthy widow, who had decided to vacation in Boston, left her Negro maid Clara and the maid's husband John in charge of the house. Clara decided that while the owner was away she would take in washing to make a little money. John, returning home from work one day, saw a white man leaving by the back door and suspected the worst of his wife. Later, when he confronted Clara with his accusation, she accused him of the same infidelity. One word led to another, and in the heat of the argument John stabbed her in the throat. Running to escape his knife, she started up the stairs, but the loss of blood was too much; she slumped, falling backward like a heap of wet wash to the bottom of the stairs.

Realizing what he had done, John grabbed her by the hair of the head and pulled her into the kitchen where he tried to finish his job, but she revived and with the strength of desperation pulled the china closet to the floor. This only infuriated John more, and with one quick swipe of the knife he completely cut her head from her body. Later he threw the head into the coal-burning cookstove and dismembered the rest of her body. Several years later he was convicted and executed for his wife's murder.

27

After recounting this story, the former renter declared vehemently that his family was unable to live in the house. Footsteps, groans, and shrieks filled the night with horror. My grandfather thought this was nonsense and said so in no uncertain terms.

The first night he and his family lived in the house they thought they heard steps in the hallway. Each night the sounds increased in volume until at last no one could sleep unless the gas lights were left burning in the hall. Also, no one could sleep in the bedroom where Clara had once slept because the blankets would not stay on the bed. Grandfather was a stubborn man and determined not to let these strange happenings ruin his investment. He was convinced that there was a logical explanation.

Several months later, during a hot summer night, a gust of wind blew out all the gas lights. Before anyone could relight them, shuffling steps were heard on the stairs, a loud crash came from the kitchen, and sounds followed as if every dish in the house was being broken. Horrible screams came from one of the bedrooms. Several minutes later grandfather's sister was found lying on the floor in Clara's bedroom; her nightgown had been stripped from her body, and great welts — some as big as a thumb — covered her entire torso. She said that she had been beaten with a blacksnake whip.

Even Yankee thrift could not withstand this incident. Soon afterwards the house was left vacant, and one night it mysteriously burned to the ground.

12: The Mysterious Music

Several years ago near the small town of Cottageville an elderly engineer died. The old man had lived in a small house approximately two miles down the track from the town, and it was fairly well concealed by the heavy woods.

It was said that the old engineer had been very fond of the Christmas season and was always singing carols and buying the smaller children candy. It was also said that he had one possession of which he was really proud — an old phonograph with some old-time records, mostly of Christmas carols.

In the summer of 1968 the Baltimore and Ohio Railroad Company took up the tracks outside of Cottageville so they could be put to use elsewhere. After the tracks were removed, hunters found that the track bed provided good access to the thicker parts of the woods. During the track-lifting process, the house where the old man had lived was completely destroyed.

Two days before Christmas, Bill Johnson was driving out the track bed when he heard what he described as music blowing through the trees. He turned off the motor so he could hear more clearly. When he tried to start the car again, the starter wouldn't even turn the engine over. Then Bill saw a man walk across the track bed and go into an old house on the other side, and at the same time the music began to grow softer. Then, all of a sudden, the music stopped and at the same moment the house and the man vanished.

Bill said he was scared to death and knew he had to get

out of there. To his relief, now his car started as easily as it ever did. It has been said by elderly neighbors that the old engineer always insisted that any visitor listen to his records. If a person didn't, the old man considered it an insult.

The next night thirteen boys in three cars went to the same place Bill had gone. They turned off their motors and had been waiting there for about fifteen minutes when a strange, disturbing type of music became audible. It sounded as if it were coming right through the trees or perhaps out of them. It was just as Bill had described except for the fact that neither the man nor the house appeared to them. But they did hear the music, and none of the cars would start until the music had stopped.

This happened on the evening before Christmas Day, and it never happened on the nights that followed. Everything mysterious stopped when Christmas had passed, but there will be another Christmas, and the boys plan to investigate further.

13: The Last Lodge of Ravenswood

During my last year in high school I worked part-time in the local movie theater. I ran the projector and swept the place out at night. I had not worked there quite three months when I witnessed a most frightening sight. I was alone in the theater and had finished my work. I was

30

about to walk down the aisle and check the fire exit to make sure it was locked, when something passed behind the screen, carrying what seemed to be a lantern. I stopped dead still and watched the figure walk across the stage and disappear on the other side. I was too frightened to follow, so I made my way cautiously to the ticket booth and telephoned the police. I then called my employer and reported an apparent burglar. She told me to wait outside until she got there.

I had been outside only a few minutes when the police arrived. I again explained what I had seen and they proceeded to search the entire theater. Their search brought no results and they even hinted that maybe I had just thought I'd seen something. As they started to leave I asked them if they had checked the rear door. They said the rear door was locked. The theater is housed in one of the oldest buildings in Ravenswood, and the doors can only be locked from the inside, unless you have a key. I had the only key to the rear exit in my pocket.

When my employer arrived, I told her that the police had searched the place and found nothing. I also told her that the rear door had been locked at the time I saw the burglar. She didn't seem a bit surprised and told me she believed my story of what I had seen. Her attitude toward the situation seemed strange to me, and I asked her if she was worried about the person who was now locked inside the theater. She told me she wasn't, because the same person had been there for thirty years.

I had always considered my employer a level-headed woman and her statement confused me completely. It was at this point that she began relating to me the story of Ravenswood's "Last Lodge." She started out by telling me that I was not the first person who had sighted the figure in the theater. Many of her workers had seen him in the past.

Many years ago there was a lodge hall in Ravenswood on the second floor of the building adjoining the theater. The full history of the lodge was not known because the membership and its activities were shrouded in secrecy. The biggest mystery seemed to center around the initiation ceremonies. Prospective members were expected to stay all night in the attic of the lodge. It is not certain exactly what went on during the night, but it is known that many men refused to stay in their confinement for the full length of time. There was even an attempt to evict the group, but their lease was legal and binding.

The order came to an abrupt end when the building was gutted by fire one night during an initiation. All the members escaped but one. The man in the attic, where the fire is believed to have originated, was not found. No legal proceedings could be brought against the group or its leaders, because of lack of evidence. The building has since been restored but the lodge has never again held a meeting.

I asked my employer if she believed the figure I had seen to be the man lost in the fire. She told me she was sure of it. She explained that before the fire, the buildings had been connected, instead of being separated as they now were by a brick wall. She also told me that there were still a few passages that connected the buildings. I asked her if she had ever seen the figure herself, and a look of pain came over her face. She said she had — many times. I asked her if she believed it to be a ghost. She said that she did.

I thought for a moment that she was out of her mind. I had always thought of her as a smart business woman.

Now she seemed to be acting like a superstitious old fool. I didn't believe a word she had told me.

When I got home that night I asked my father if a lodge had really existed in that building. I decided not to tell him about what I had seen that night. He seemed reluctant to discuss the subject, but after some persistence on my part, he began to speak. He confirmed the fact that a lodge had existed and that a fire had occurred. I was so amazed that I asked him about a man being lost in the fire. This he also confirmed.

I then told him about my employer believing that the man lost in the fire was still roaming the building in spirit form. He asked me what had led me to this subject and I told him about what I had seen. His face seemed to freeze and he said nothing for a few moments. I told him I didn't believe my employer's story because she had seemed so certain of the presence of the person. She seemed almost to have contact with him. It was at this time my father told me something that I hadn't known before. The man lost in the fire was my employer's husband.

The theater has since been closed, but the building remains.

14: The Farmhouse Ghost

My aunt went to visit some of her relatives in Saint Claire, Ohio, arriving there from West Virginia in the evening at about seven o'clock. After having a late supper and chat with the family, she decided to go to bed, because she was very tired. This happened at the turn of the century, and traveling such a distance at that time was more tiring than it would be today.

She had been asleep for about five hours when she was suddenly awakened by a strange noise. She opened her eyes and looked around. The image of a man grasping a bloody club in his right hand was walking toward her. The next instant he disappeared.

My aunt didn't scream for help, thinking that she was just dreaming because of her exhaustion. She closed her eyes and fell asleep once again.

After supper the following evening, the family gathered by the fireplace for a quiet evening. My aunt's Uncle Harry began to tell ghost stories. He told everyone that the house they were now sitting in was believed to be haunted. Everyone became interested, so he told them the story he knew.

Fifteen years before, a family named Walker lived in the huge old farmhouse. They were an eccentric family, who never got along very well together. Mr. Walker had mental problems that no one knew about until one day he took a "fit" and clubbed his wife to death while she was sleeping.

The murder occurred in the bedroom now being occupied by my aunt, and it was said that Mr. Walker's ghost

34

often returned to the scene of the murder he committed. One other family had lived in the house before my aunt's relatives moved in, and their older daughter claimed to have seen his ghost return.

My aunt couldn't believe what she had heard. She had deliberately failed to mention what she had seen to anyone. Now she explained to the family that she had seen a mysterious apparition the night before. They told her that she was probably dreaming, but to this day she sincerely believes she saw Mr. Walker's ghost at the old farmhouse.

15: The Wealthy Widower

In the small community of Glenfalls, a huge white mansion surrounded by pine trees stands on a lonely hill. A legend accompanies this strange but stately dwelling, which is now empty and weather-beaten.

The land around the house was once owned by a wealthy widower and his son. Being a very miserly and conservative fellow, the widower lived in a small log cabin where the present mansion is situated. He was obsessed by the lust for money, and he kept all his treasures in a locked box under his bed. Money became so important to him that he found it difficult to trust his own son. His son, an easy-going young man of twenty, did not miss the joys of wealth.

The widower's love of money finally drove him to his grave. His mind had grown weak from worry and the fear of being separated from his precious box. Before he died he buried his money under the floor of his log cabin.

The widower left a will giving all his land to his only son, but the clever man had made one stipulation; his son was not to tear down the little log cabin. The son could build anywhere else on the land, but the cabin was to remain where it was.

A few years after the death of his father, the young man married a girl from a nearby town and took his bride to live in the cabin on the hill. His wife, a prominent figure in society, despised living in the dingy cabin and urged him to tear it down and replace it with a house that was suitable to their position.

After much begging and pleading, the young man finally consented. While the cabin was being taken down, the money was discovered under the floorboard where the widower had left it. All the money was used to build the most extravagant house in the area.

When the building was completed, the wife decided to give a party in order to show off their new home. The party was a success, and the guests were astonished by the beauty of the mansion.

After the guests left, the proud owners soon retired. They locked the doors to their mansion, fearing that someone might steal their rich possessions.

In the morning the mistress of the house found the front door standing open. Amazed by the scene, she ran to awaken her husband. He was terrified to think that someone had come in during the night. They searched the house and found nothing missing. Only a rug in the middle of the floor had been turned wrong side up.

The next two nights the same thing happened. Then the husband decided to stay awake to catch their prowler

36

in the act. He sat in a chair near the door with his gun in hand until the hour of twelve without hearing or seeing anything. He finally tired of the game and started up the stairs to his room.

Just then he heard footsteps outside. The door jarred and the locks fell free. As the door swung open, the figure of his father appeared in the doorway. In his panic, the young man shot the image and it disappeared. Terrified by the thought of killing his own father, he turned the gun to himself and fired.

His wife, standing at the top of the stairs, had witnessed the scene. She was found beside the body of her husband in a state of delirium.

The house still stands on the hill in Glenfalls, West Virginia.

16: The Ghost of Hangman's Hollow

In the 1920s, there was a vicious moonshiner in the area of Gilman, West Virginia, near Elkins, who had declared war on government agents or "revenooers." Every time one would come around any of his stills, he would barbarously murder him and then dismember the body and cremate the remains in a furnace used to make charcoal for the stills.

This went on for several years, but finally the murderer was caught by a group of federal men, who had combined

their forces to avenge all the agents who had been murdered while doing their duty.

Since it was almost dark when they made their capture, the agents decided to wait until morning to transport the prisoner to a federal jail. They placed the moonshiner in an outbuilding and left one man on guard, while the rest went to bed.

The next morning the "revenooers" found their fellow worker lying unconscious outside the shed, which was empty. Immediately they started to comb the nearby woods for their prisoner. About noon one of them gave a signal shot, and they all gathered quickly. Down in a pitlike hollow, hanging from a moss-covered grapevine, was the man for whom they were searching. Evidently he had tripped and fallen into the ravine, where a vine had encircled his neck and broken it. Thus ended the life of a murderer.

After this, the local residents stated that each time they passed that hollow they could hear a moaning noise. They said it was the voice of the moonshiner crying in pain.

17: The Haunted Field

My grandfather tells a strange story about a piece of land he had received from his father and later had given in turn to my uncle. One day grandfather and I were crossing Uncle Roy's meadow, which had been grown up in weeds for as long as I could remember. As I walked through the tall grass, I stumbled on a rock; I examined it more closely and saw it was a rough, handmade tombstone.

"Yes," grandfather answered my questioning look, "this meadow's full of them; that's why we don't plow it, although one person — my father — tried."

I wanted to know more, so we sat on a fence half the afternoon while grandfather told me about the haunted field.

Long ago a slave trader had made his home on this property. He was a cruel man, and his neighbors gave him a wide berth. He had built a rough sort of barracks against the hillside where the slaves were kept chained to the walls, and in the field below he buried the bodies of those who tried to escape, or were disobedient, as a warning to the others. This man enjoyed torturing his victims before killing them, however, and when it got so bad that the good people of Green Valley drove him out, no one would buy his land because of the evil name attached to it.

After several years, my great-grandfather bought it, against the advice of his neighbors, and tried to remove all the taint from it. He burned the decaying slavehouse and after about thirty years of living on the property, decided to use the meadow where the slaves had been buried.

Grandfather was a little boy then, but he could remember his father saying that he had had a strange sense of foreboding all during the plowing and that the horses had shied and given him a great deal of trouble all afternoon.

The family all went to bed with the sun that night, because there was so much to do the next morning. Grandfather was awakened by his father's terrified screams. His father had seen something – or maybe dreamed it, but it was real to him. He had heard chains clanking, moans and screams of tortured slaves, and had heard their quiet cries of despair. "Let us have peace, at least in our graves," they begged, crawling on their knees, their chains clanking.

Grandfather stopped there and lit his pipe, but after a time he went on.

"Well, my pa heard that carrying on for about a week; then he decided he didn't really need that field. He let it grow back up, and he didn't hear any more strange noises. I left that meadow alone too, and so did your Uncle Roy."

"The screams and chain-clanking," I said, "all this was just your father's conscience bothering him in the form of a dream."

Grandfather took another puff; then he said quietly, "But all us kids, we heard it too!"

18: The Misty Ghost

Many years ago, a young woman from Rowlesburg was working in the city of Pittsburgh as a domestic. While there, she happened to meet a young man from Manheim, a small community across the river from Rowlesburg.

They both were lonely, and before long they became good friends. They spent many a long evening talking of their families and their mutual friends. This relationship blossomed into love – at least on the girl's part. But in

41

spite of his avowed sentiments the young man refused to marry her. All too soon she lost her position, and there was nothing left for her but to return home.

As she rode back on the train, all she could think of was the disgrace she would bring to her family. She was not even sure that they would let her in.

Each mile bringing her closer home seemed to make her burn deeper and deeper with shame, and with the excuse that she needed air, she went out to the platform between the cars.

The night was beautiful, with a full moon, and she noticed that the train was now on a high winding trail, following Cheat River. Just as the train passed over the caverns, she jumped.

The young man, hearing of her death, hurried home. Filled with shame and remorse, he went to the caves on the anniversary of her death. He never came back. Two days later, he was found on the bottom of the river, directly opposite the place where she had jumped.

The old-timers say that on the night of the full moon, her spirit rises above the place where she jumped — and hovers, waiting. Another white mist rises from the river and comes to meet it. They merge, then drift upward and fade away.

19: The Murdered Girl

Many years ago a wealthy Connecticut man had a brother who lived on Point Mountain in Webster County, West Virginia. The wealthy man's daughter was stricken by that dreaded disease called consumption, and he wrote his brother asking if she could come to the West Virginia farm to spend a month or two, for the doctor had said that a change of climate might cure her.

The brother agreed to take her, and preparations for the visit were made. When the girl arrived, she paid $1,500 in advance for her board, room, and expenses. Later her father sent her $2,000 more, which she gave to her uncle to keep for her. He decided to kill her and leave with her money. After the murder, he buried her under the hearthstone of the fireplace. He then took her money and went West.

The house was haunted after this happened, and the door wouldn't stay shut. Occupants even tried bolting it, but to no avail. No one would live there any length of time. Two old Christian ladies who lived nearby told the man who owned the house that if he would put a bed in the room where the ghost was and get wood enough to burn all night, they would come and sleep in the bed, and when the ghost appeared, they would ask it what it wanted.

The owner prepared the room as they suggested. That night they were lying there talking when the door opened and a young girl walked in. She put her hands behind her back and turned around, facing the old women. They raised up on their elbows and asked her what she wanted.

43

She said, "I was a rich man's daughter. My uncle killed me for my money and buried me under this hearthstone. If you'll look, you'll find me."

The next morning they told a neighbor, who lifted the hearthstone and found her body. They called the authorities, who got out a warrant for the uncle's arrest, brought him back from the West, and hanged him on a tree near where he had killed the girl.

20: The Hitchhiking Ghost of Buttermilk Hill

In the early 1900s an old-time peddler traveled from Fairmont to Fairview, with his heavy pack of goods on his back. Everyone liked him and seemed happy to have him come – not only to display his wares but also to report any news.

The peddler was such a good, kind, and interesting man that people missed him when he stopped coming. It seemed as if he had disappeared. No one had heard or seen anything of him until finally his body was found stuck in a barrel which had been rolled into the valley below Buttermilk Hill.

On dark, dreary nights, people would stay away from this hill. They tried to pass over it before dark, because it was said that when one came to the top of the hill, the peddler's ghost would ride with him in his buckboard wagon or buggy, or behind him on his horse, until he arrived at the first house at the foot of the hill.

Jack Toothman, who worked in the mines at Grant Town, always rode a brown mare between the mines and his house at Monumental. He usually tried to cross the hill before dark, but one night he stopped at a bar in Grant Town. There he started drinking and talking with some of his friends, and before he knew it, darkness had appeared. That night Jack met the ghost of Buttermilk Hill.

Sometime later, neighbors were awakened by a pounding at their door. When the husband opened the door, he saw Jack standing on the porch. He was as white as a sheet and shaking all over, so frightened he could hardly talk. He swore that the ghost had jumped on his horse behind him, wrapped its cold arms around his waist, and ridden with him until he got to the bottom of the hill. He said he had fought with it all the way down the hill, but could not get it off until he reached the bottom. From that time on he always made sure to get past the hill before dark.

21: Midnight Whippoorwill

During Prohibition many stills and moonshiners were to be found in West Virginia. One particular still was located in Smith Hollow. The owner was Charley Smut, a very eccentric man. Charley was a bachelor and had only one good friend — Jim Hayward. The two lived together in an old weather-beaten shack at the head of Smith Hollow.

Jim was the only person who knew about Charley's still. Charley would only go to the still at midnight, while Jim stood watch. They had an understanding that if Jim saw someone coming, he would whistle like a whippoorwill. On several occasions they used this signal.

Every night after Charley had finished working with the still, he and Jim would sit down by the oak tree where Jim had stood watch and drink their daily portion of moonshine from tin cups that were camouflaged and hidden each night in a big hole in the oak tree. Jim thought that Charley always got the biggest portion and was bitter about this, but he never said anything because he thought Charley wouldn't let him have any more liquor.

Jim was becoming very old and feeble. On a snowy and windy Friday night he died. Now Charley was all alone, but he never failed to make his midnight excursions to the still. One week after Jim had died, something very unusual happened during Charley's trip. He heard a familiar sound — the whippoorwill. Immediately, he blew out the light in the lantern and hid. After a few minutes, he called, "Jim, Jim! Is that you, Jim?"

In return, Charley heard the sound of the whippoorwill and the clatter of tin cups. Then all was silent. Every Friday night the same thing occurred.

On the first anniversary of Jim's death, Charley made his usual trip to the still, but this time something else happened. After hearing the usual clatter of tin cups and the whippoorwill, Charley glanced over to the oak tree. To his amazement, there stood Jim with a tin cup in his hand.

"I finally got my share of moonshine!" Jim said, and then he disappeared with the tin cup in his hand.

Charley was terrified and ran to his cabin. But after that time, he never again heard the whippoorwill or the clatter of tin cups, and he never again saw Jim.

22: Galloping Horses

During the Civil War, when West Virginia was often overrun by both Confederate and Union troops, a father and his two sons went off to fight in the army, leaving the wife and daughter at home alone. Before leaving, the three men took all of the money and buried it, never telling the rest of the family where, for fear the women might be forced by enemy soldiers to surrender it. The men, of course, believed that at least one of them would get back alive.

It so happened that all three men died in the war and none were left to return home. The two lonely women continued to live in their remote country home. Every night they would hear horses galloping around and around the house, but when they looked outside, nothing could be seen. Finally, the mother could stand it no longer, so she and the daughter would walk to a nearby farmhouse to sleep each night, returning early in the morning to tend the farm. No matter how hard they tried, things seemed to go from bad to worse, and the two women were having a very difficult time making ends meet.

One evening when the two women were preparing to leave for the night, a peddler arrived and asked for a night's lodging. The women explained that they did not stay in the house at night because of strange noises, but he was welcome to sleep there if he wished. The peddler was quite tired and accepted their offer, telling them he had no fears.

As soon as the women were gone, the peddler prepared himself for the night. He covered the fire in the fireplace, took off his boots, and lay down on a cot near the fire. Soon he was fast asleep.

About midnight he was awakened by the sound of horses galloping down the road. He thought this unusual in such a remote area and at such a late hour, but he was even more surprised when they galloped up to the house and around it. He quickly went to the window, drew aside the curtain, and looked out into a clear moonlit night. He saw no sign of horses. He lay down again and soon dozed off, only to be awakened by the same sound, louder and closer than before.

The peddler now began to be frightened, so he latched the door tightly and pushed heavy bureaus and other furniture against it. Again he lay down, feeling more secure.

Suddenly the galloping stopped and the door opened as easily as if it had not been barred. An old man with a long beard entered the room and sat near the fire, looking into the coals. The peddler noticed that the old man's throat was cut from ear to ear. He could not keep from asking, "Old man, do you know your throat is cut?"

The old man answered without looking up, "Yes, I know my throat is cut." And then he continued to look into the fire.

About this time a second man, younger than the first, walked through the door. He too sat looking into the fire, and he too had his throat cut. The peddler finally asked him the same question and received the same reply. Soon a third man entered the room in the same condition, and he too sat staring into the fire. He gave the same answer to the peddler's question that the other two had given.

After some time had passed, the peddler asked who they were. The old man explained that they were the men of that particular household, who had been killed in battle by having their throats cut. He said they could not rest until the money they had hidden was back in the hands of the two women who needed it so desperately. They wanted to show him where they had hidden the money and asked him to give it to the wife and daughter.

The peddler promised that he would put it in their hands, and the ghosts proceeded to lead the way to the fence corner where the money was buried. But upon leaving, the three men warned him that if he did not give the money to the women to whom it belonged, he would never sleep another night, but would always hear the galloping horses. They also told him to tell the wife and daughter that they need not leave the house again, since they would never be bothered by the sounds of galloping horses after that night. Then the three men rode away.

The peddler kept his word and gave the money to the women as he had promised and was rewarded handsomely. From that time on, the women stayed in their home and never heard the sound of horses galloping around the house again.

23: A Confederate Soldier

One of the best-known ghost tales of Tucker County was told by Lewis Kittle, who lived on the Indian Fork of Clover Run. His reputation among his neighbors and acquaintances was above reproach, and the following story is an account of the facts as he knew and understood them. Mr. Kittle was not a superstitious man and was not a believer in spiritualism.

In 1867 Lewis Kittle, with several others, was mining coal near the ground on which the battle of Rich Mountain was fought. He and a cousin named Daniel Courtright boarded with a Mr. Hart, whose house was adjacent to the battlefield and had been used as a hospital during the battle. In the course of the battle a soldier had been shot in the room later occupied by Kittle and his cousin. The first night in the room they heard a weird and continuous noise. They supposed it was only the wind, but one day they were told by a fellow miner that the room was haunted.

One Saturday night soon after this, Courtright was absent, and Kittle slept in the room alone. Along in the night he was awakened by a strange coldness and a dim light that outlined the furniture in the misty air. The silence was broken only occasionally by a low sound that seemed to be the echo of a night breeze. Drawn by some unseen, irresistible power, Kittle arose from the bed and moved near the door. He said that he felt no fear and was struck with a sense of solemnity. Almost immediately he saw eight forms materialize, clad in Confederate uniforms. Silently they approached the bed on which Kittle had been sleeping and removed the covers, throwing them over the footboard. Four of them leaned over the bed and raised something up, as if lifting a weight.

The object, which Kittle could not see, was laid down carefully upon apparently nothing. Two of those who had lifted the object from the bed then took a place in front of the four, and the other two stepped behind. In this order they slowly marched toward the door, and as they filed out, Kittle saw lying between the pallbearers the body of a handsome young man. His coat and vest had been removed, but he was wearing butternut trousers. The figures made no sound until they had reached the hallway, where a noise resembling the knock of a crutch on a wooden floor was heard. This was followed by the closing of a door.

Kittle collected the covers and returned to bed. He said that there was not any possibility of his being mistaken about what he saw. He was in perfect health, wide awake, and not frightened. Kittle spoke to several men staying in the house who said that other people who had occupied the room had had similar experiences.

On another occasion, when Mr. Courtright was present, the covers were removed from the bed several times in quick succession. Finally, both men got up, clutching their bedclothes tightly. The same cold, clammy light entered the room and the weird wind was again heard as the two men were pushed out of the way and up against the wall. Then a calm and quiet settled over the room, and the gray air rolled like a fog in a slight breeze. The forms began to emerge slowly at first and then suddenly stood in bold view. Again they approached the bed. In a few moments they solemnly took up their burden and enacted the same scene.

These nocturnal visits became so frequent that Kittle and Courtright finally got used to it. When they first became aware of the cold light and weird echo, they would wrap their blankets tightly around them and say, "Here come them rebels again."

24: Return from Death

When the war started in 1861, the only son in a family that lived near my great-grandparents went off to fight in the Confederate army. The mother and three daughters were left to manage the farm, as the father had been killed in an accident the year before.

They were at home one afternoon when a Union soldier galloped up to the house and knocked. Without opening the door, Mrs. Adams asked what he wanted. He demanded entrance into the house, saying that he would shoot through the windows if she didn't open up. There was nothing to do except to let him in.

He asked the girls where the watches and jewelry were kept. They replied that everything had been taken earlier. This statement enraged the soldier and he became nasty about the whole affair. He said he could wait as long as they could. He ordered the women to cook him a hearty supper. This he enjoyed very much since it had been a long time since he had had a good meal.

He kept the mother and her daughters prisoners the rest of that day. The following day they still insisted that their jewelry had been stolen at the outbreak of the war.

Actually, the women had hidden the valuables so they couldn't be found.

The soldier said he was tired of playing games. He would leave without hurting them if they gave the jewelry to him. Otherwise, he would have no other choice but to kill them.

Stubbornly, the women refused. Without the watches and valuables, they would have nothing left. They couldn't work the farm by themselves, so the jewelry was the only security they had.

As the soldier prepared to carry out his threat and was raising his gun, the figure of a man appeared out of nowhere, standing between the man and the women. Obviously it was no ordinary person. Although the soldier could see through the form, he could make out the features plainly. The form told the soldier to leave at once if he valued his life.

The women were speechless, for they recognized the figure as the dead husband and father. The soldier ran out the door and rode off as fast as he could. The form left as quietly and silently as it had come.

Each of the women thought she had imagined the whole affair, but all soon realized that the father had come back to save them from death.

25: A Face in the Window

During Civil War days, Charles Perry, a soldier in the Union army, was often sent out to get supplies for the hospitals — butter, eggs, milk, chickens, and so on — and had many interesting experiences. One morning when he started out to gather supplies, he came to a farmhouse situated near a small creek.

He rode up to the place, hitched his horse to the post, and knocked on the door. After a few minutes he decided no one was home, but as he was going down the steps, he saw someone peering out the second-floor window.

Charles went back up to the porch and pushed open the door, gun in hand. There by the chimney stood a middle-aged lady, as white as a ghost. He asked her why she hadn't answered the door, and she replied that she was afraid he would kill her, since he was a Union soldier. Remembering the face at the window upstairs, he asked if anyone else was in the house. She swore to him that they were alone, but he asked if he could look around. Although she said she would rather he left, he started upstairs.

Slowly he climbed the steps, expecting a Confederate soldier to jump out of a doorway to shoot him at any moment. He ventured first into one room and then another. Finding no one, he had almost decided that he had imagined the face at the window.

Suddenly, out of the corner of his eye he saw the figure of a young woman slide into an opening in the wall. The girl had long brown hair and a beautiful complexion. She wore a pink silk dress that fell in folds around her legs. As he turned toward her, the opening in the wall closed and, upon inspection, could not be found. Thinking it could be a passage to an inner room of the house, he closely examined the wood. There was not even a crack in the wall!

Bewildered, he went to find the woman he had spoken with, but when he returned to the first floor of the house, she was nowhere in sight. Searching the house carefully, he could find no trace of her anywhere. Knowing she couldn't have gone far, he looked around the farm, but could find no clue to her disappearance.

He rode to the nearest farmhouse, and a lady came out on the porch to greet him. He asked who lived in the farmhouse to the south, and she replied that the place had been deserted since an intoxicated Union soldier had come upon the house where the mother and daughter lived alone. The soldier had taken both their lives when they would not give him food and money! Shocked, he asked the housewife to describe the mother and daughter. Her descriptions fit the women he had seen exactly.

Charles rode back to the house in hopes of seeing the beautiful girl again. A strange feeling seemed to attract him to the place. Upon entering, he saw for the first time that the rooms were filled with dust and cobwebs, as if no one had been in the house for months. All he could see were his own footprints leading up the stairs.

26: A Ghostly Avenger

In the southern part of West Virginia there is a gravestone with the following inscription: "SACRED TO THE MEMORY OF JIM BROWN." There is no date, no epitaph, because Jim Brown was hanged. This is the story.

At the close of the Civil War, a company of Federal soldiers was stationed in Marion County. Charles Murphy was a lieutenant in this company. His brother, who was an officer quartered in a neighboring county, was sent one day to receive funds for the payment of some men. After he had received the money, he set out again, planning to return to his troops by evening.

That night Charles Murphy was awakened by a violent flapping of his tent. It sounded as if a gale were coming, but when he arose to make sure that the pegs and poles of his tent were secure, the noise ceased, and he was surprised to find that the air was calm. When he returned to bed, the flapping began again, and this time he dressed himself and went outside to make a better examination.

In the shadow of a nearby tree, a man stood beckoning. It was his brother. In a low, grave voice he told Charles to follow him. The lieutenant walked swiftly through the woods for some time with his brother until they descended a slope to the edge of a swamp, where he stumbled against something. Looking down at the object on which he had tripped, he saw it was his brother's corpse — not newly dead, but cold and rigid. The pockets had been rifled and the clothing was soaked with mire and blood.

Dazed and terrified, he returned to camp where he

roused some of his men. At daybreak they secured the body.

It was not long before evidence turned up that brought about the arrest of Jim Brown. There was a hint that his responsibility for the crime was revealed through the same supernatural being that had warned Lieutenant Murphy. Brown was an ignorant farmer who hated Yankee soldiers and who had been excited by learning the officer was carrying money.

He had offered to take his victim by a shortcut to his camp, but took him into the swamp instead, where he shot him and robbed him.

27: Darkish Knob

Near the town of Parsons, West Virginia, there is a tall, steep hill covered almost entirely with loose rock. Only one path leads over this hill, and it is almost impassable. The hill is called Darkish Knob.

During the Civil War the underground railroad was bringing as many Negro slaves as possible to the North where they would be free. These slaves had to travel by night so they wouldn't be seen, and they would hide at different houses during the day. They could not travel the same routes many times because the authorities would wait there to capture them.

One of the most favored areas to travel through was the mountainous region of West Virginia. There were many hiding places, but traveling by night was extremely

dangerous. The few trails that the Negroes dared to travel were so perilous that few people would attempt them by day.

One of the resting places for these fugitives was a house in a valley at the foot of Darkish Knob. It was well hidden by mountains on all four sides. In fact, the valley was so very well hidden that the Negroes themselves often could not find it.

A young Negro girl was trying to locate this place one dark night. She was being chased by men her owner had hired to catch his runaway slaves. She missed the valley and started up the path over Darkish Knob. Her horse was very tired, but she pushed him on harder. The top of this hill drops straight down to Cheat River. As she reached the top, she turned to look back. Her horse lost his footing, and both horse and rider rolled down the hill and hit the sharp rocks in the river. As the girl dropped, her scream was heard for miles. This hill has been known as Darkish Knob since that time.

The girl's ghost is said to have returned to the top of this hill every year on the eve of the date of her death. It chants and moans over the death just as the Negro people once did when one of their people died. At exactly the instant of the fatal plunge the ghost screams, loud and long.

The young people in this area say that the chanting and moaning is only the wind in the trees. They also say that the scream is that of a wildcat. But the older generation know that this is the ghost of the young Negro girl.

28: A Slave Boy's Revenge

It was very late at night as young Curt, a slave boy, slipped through the fence surrounding the small, dirt-floored shack he was forced to call his home. After a very hard day in the fields, he decided he could stand it no longer. He was willing to risk death itself rather than continue life under these wretched conditions. He made his break through the open fields and into the woods unseen.

His break was not discovered until the next morning. Upon learning of the boy's escape, the master immediately went for his bloodhounds, which quickly picked up the trail and sped, barking, into the woods. Curt, being on foot, had been unable to cover a great distance, even though he had several hours' head start.

When he heard the hounds in the distance, he decided to backtrack to a swamp near the plantation. As he neared the swamp, the dogs had closed the gap to just a few hundred yards. He began to run with all his strength across an open field that lay between him and the swamp.

He was caught by the dogs in the center of the field and was badly torn up by the time the master got to him, but he was still very much conscious. As the master arrived, he called off the dogs, and in front of many a watching slave (for the field was in sight of the huts) he drew his sword and with one mighty blow cut off the young boy's head.

After that, the master couldn't sleep, for he kept hearing strange sounds — as if someone were trying to enter his bedroom. This went on for several nights. One night he heard the voice of the young boy he had brutally killed. He began following it and eventually was led back to the field where he had killed young Curt. Some of the slaves saw him as he passed.

Suddenly a loud scream was heard. As the rest of the whites rushed into the field, they saw a horrible sight. The master lay dead in the same spot where Curt had lain. To their surprise, they noticed he had no head, and beside the body lay the very same sword he had used to murder the slave boy. There were no tracks to be picked up by the dogs, and the mystery was never solved.

29: Frist House

During the Civil War, Hardy County was one of the few counties in West Virginia to go Confederate. The reason Hardy turned rebel was that several well-to-do farmers in the county used slave labor. The only important person opposed to the Confederacy was John Frist, an influential man who lived in a large house outside of Moorefield. Because of John's resistance, a group of hotheaded rebels went to his house one night and murdered him, his wife, and their three children.

After this, John Frist's home was used as a prison for runaway slaves who were caught. The slaves would be taken into the basement of the house, chained to the wall, and left for dead. Those who performed these acts of insanity were called the McNeil Rangers, and they operated out of Moorefield.

After the South's surrender the slaves in Hardy County were released — all except the ones who had died in the cellar of their prison. A group of townspeople went to the Frist house and cleared out the bones and decaying bodies.

This house is still standing and is in very good condition. Several families have owned or rented it since the end of the Civil War but none of them has remained in it for more than a year. I know of five families — all from other places — that have owned it in my lifetime. The families that have lived there claim that once a year, on the anniversary of the Frist family's murder, blood appears on the floor and walls of the room in which they were killed. It slowly wears off during the year, but it can't be painted over or sanded out. Also strange screams and the sound of chains rattling come from the cellar.

All my life I have heard that this house is haunted; I hope it does not carry a curse, because my parents rented it for a few months, about a year after they were married, and I was born there.

30: The Murdered Prisoner's Ghost

About 1900, the Hall family lived near a so-called haunted hollow on a farm in Pendleton County. Their house was on one side of a dirt road, and on the other side stood two hills with a hollow between them. About halfway up the hollow stood an old log cabin.

The story was told that the log cabin in the hollow was used as a jail during the Civil War. One day an inmate dressed in white (probably his underwear) tried to escape. He ran as far as one of the hills, but was shot. Blood poured out of his right leg and stained his white pants. He reeled around, stretching forth his arm in a gesture of surrender, but was shot in the other leg. Blood also poured from his left leg. He was carried into the cabin, dead. It is not known whether he was buried or not.

As the years passed, the cabin decayed, the roof fell in, and the area around it was grown over with brush. But when people passed by the cabin, they could hear the cries of anguish and moaning.

When Mrs. Hall moved into this area, she knew the hollow was supposed to be haunted, but she did not know the story of the prisoner. The Hall family grazed their cattle on one side of the hill, and it was Mrs. Hall's chore to bring them home every evening.

One evening a few cattle strayed up beyond the cabin. In taking a short cut, Mrs. Hall passed the cabin and heard the moans. She was not a woman to be easily frightened and called out in a loud voice, "I've heard there are ghosts in the hollow. If you're a ghost, come out! I'm not afraid. And, if you're a man, come out. I'm still not afraid."

But the noise that followed did frighten her. Hearing a loud rumbling, as if someone were removing debris, she ran down the hill towards her nearest neighbors. As she ran, she turned to see a man dressed in white, with two bloodstained legs, standing on the hill with his arm raised.

She finally arrived at her neighbors' house and told of her experience. The woman then related the legend and upon hearing this, Mrs. Hall fainted. Mr. Hall was sent for – to take his wife home – and, as they passed the foot of the hollow on their journey homeward, Mrs. Hall fainted again. The strain of living in that location was so great for Mrs. Hall that the family was forced to move.

31: The Cole Mountain Light

Outside of Moorefield, West Virginia, stands Cole Mountain. This area was the scene of a strange happening, back in the mid-1800s.

Charles Jones, a large landowner, took one of his most faithful slaves and went coon hunting one night. The slave was carrying a lantern that provided the two with some light while they were following the voices of the dogs. Suddenly the dogs began barking more fiercely. Since this meant they probably had treed a coon, Charles and the slave both took off running in the direction of the barking. The slave was younger and stronger than his master, so he led with the lantern. When he arrived at the place where the dogs were, he discovered that the master was nowhere in sight. The Negro, who was a loyal friend as well as a faithful servant, waited for a while and then went searching for his master. He hunted all through the night and the next morning, but could find no trace of his friend.

Overcome by fear, the slave went back to the house to inform the Jones family of the incident. Mrs. Jones organized a search party made up of friends and neighbors, and this group, led by the slave, covered the mountain thoroughly. After a whole week of searching, in which they hadn't found Jones or any sign of him, they gave up. The slave was never accused of harming the missing man, for everyone knew how devoted he was to his master.

The Negro kept on searching after the others stopped. Exactly one year to the night after his master had disappeared, the slave took his lantern and left for a final search. He was never seen again. But on certain nights the people who lived around Cole Mountain said they could see his lantern still patrolling the mountain. They said that after the night the slave disappeared, his lantern light slowly changed from yellow to a bright red.

Even today people still see the light — especially those who live around Moorefield. Some of them have had strange experiences with it. Charles Allen, a former teacher at Moorefield High School, saw the light from a distance and thought it was the moon shining on a stream. But the light appears on a part of the mountain where there is no stream.

Several times the light has chased hunters off the mountain. Two years ago two men from Westernport,

Maryland, were coon hunting on Cole Mountain when something frightened off their dogs. The hunters were looking for the dogs when they saw a strange red light appear a short distance in front of them. The light kept coming closer and closer. All of a sudden it let out a weird scream, and started coming at them faster than before. The men became frightened and one of them fired three times at the light with his shotgun. At that range it would have been almost impossible to miss. But the light kept coming. The men threw down their weapons and ran as fast as they could. The light chased them off the mountain and then disappeared.

On another occasion a young man took his girl friend up on the mountain at night. Shortly after they parked the car, a weird red light appeared at the window. The young man had heard of the Cole Mountain light but had never believed in it. Thinking someone was trying to play a trick on him, he threw open the door and jumped out, ready for a fight, but there was no one there that he could see — only the light hovering in midair. As he stood there, almost in a state of shock, the light came closer to him, as if to see who he was, and then disappeared.

32: The Crying Baby of Holly

During the Depression a young girl of the neighborhood around Holly River, below Diana in Webster County, gave birth to an illegitimate child. Faced with shame and the task of supporting the child, the girl decided to destroy it. She took the infant and threw it into a hogsty to be gobbled up alive by the vicious hogs, but as it crawled in the mud the hogs paid it no mind whatsoever.

Then the despairing mother took the baby down to the logging mill by the river and thrust it into the deepest water, which was behind the dam and water wheel. Of course the infant had no chance to survive – and drowned in Holly's murky millpond. Later the mother hanged herself.

Today the local farm folks in Webster County sometimes report hearing the sound of a crying baby as they pass by the deteriorating old mill late at night.

Being somewhat skeptical of such reports, I decided to find out for myself if there was any truth in the stories. Driving to the place and parking my car, I sat and waited for anything that might happen. Sitting there in the light of the full moon, I kept my eyes on the millpond, which reflected the moon's golden glow. A steady mist spiraled up out of the black depths of the ever-flowing water. It was hard to believe that I had fished in this same spot by day and found it quite beautiful in a rugged sort of way.

While thinking about the absurdity of the situation, I began to hear a faint noise. Supposing it a feeding trout, I ignored it. But the eerie wail came again, clearer than before, and I suddenly realized that the farm folks

weren't just telling a tale. When I heard the crying the third time, there was no keeping me there. Starting up my car and pulling away, I tried to put as much distance as possible between me and the "tale come true."

There may be a logical explanation for this, but I'm not going to be the one to find out.

33: A Strange Fire

In a small town in Doddridge County, West Virginia, lived a widow and her daughter. The woman had lost her husband immediately after the birth of their only child. Because there was no one to help raise the child, the widow considered her daughter a loathsome burden.

As the years passed, the child grew to be a beautiful young girl. All the young ladies of the community were envious of her popularity. But because her mother had given her no moral instruction, she knew nothing about the perils of such popularity except what other girls had told her.

One day a handsome young serviceman came into town. The beautiful young girl chanced to meet him on the street, and a romance blossomed. But like many young servicemen, all he wanted was a good time. After he had had his fling, he left town.

A few months later the girl discovered that she was carrying the soldier's child. Her mother soon knew it too and was enraged. She condemned her daughter for the very things she had failed to warn her against.

The widow, terrified that someone might hear about the girl, locked her daughter in a room in the attic and posted a sign on the door of the house warning that her daughter was sick with smallpox. But somehow everyone heard the news anyway, and the tale spread, as rumors do.

After the baby was born, the widow took it into another room of the attic and asphyxiated it by turning on a small gas stove near where the baby was lying. That night she carried its body to the edge of a field nearby and buried it under a fence post.

The following evening two women were walking along the road near the widow's house. As they neared the field where the baby was buried, a huge ball of fire rolled down the hillside, crossed the road and field, and stopped below the fence post. The women, startled by such a strange thing but curious too, went over to the fence where the ball of fire had stopped. By the time they reached the post, the ball of fire had disappeared, but they noticed the loose dirt at the base of the fence. One of the women dug into the soil with her hands. They found the baby's body and ran to get their husbands. When they returned with the men, the body was no longer there.

Since they had heard the rumors about the young girl, they decided to go to the house and question her. They knocked on the door, but no one answered. All the blinds were drawn and the house was locked up tight. No one ever returned to the house, but a tiny new grave was found in a church graveyard nearby.

Many children who have played near the old deserted house have said they could hear a baby crying from within, but no one ever entered.

34: Jones's Hollow

There is a small settlement near Belington called Union. It is situated on top of a hill that towers over the Tygart Valley River. There are valleys and hollows between the many hills of the region, and each hollow has its own name.

Jones's Hollow has not only a name but also a legend.

Almost seventy-five years ago, a very rough man named Abraham Jones bought some land in this area. He drank heavily and gambled with some of the lowest class of people at that time.

There was another family in the community named Johnson. Hubert Johnson was almost as vile a man as Jones. He had a daughter named Rachel. One evening during a poker game, Johnson ran out of money and, having nothing else to bet, put up his daughter as stakes. Jones won his wife Rachel on Saturday night, and they were married on Sunday.

Abraham and Rachel had three children — a girl and two boys. Each day Abraham became more harsh. He soon grew to hate his children. He hated them so much that he wanted to kill them.

One day when he was drunk, he took the three children to a cave, chained them to a wall, and left them there to die.

People believed that if a woman who was barren would hear the cries of the children, find the cave where they were chained, and free them, she would be able to have three children of her own.

More than half a century later, Russell and Laura

Coolridge moved into a cottage in Jones's Hollow. They were a happy couple except for the fact that Laura was unable to have children.

People often said that on windy nights they could still hear the cries of the forsaken Jones children, but nobody was able to find the cave.

One evening as a storm approached, Laura could hear what sounded like the cries of children. Anxious for their safety, she searched the woods surrounding the cottage. Quite by accident she came upon the cave and, by entering, freed the spirits of the children.

A year later, Laura had her first child.

35: Who Was Guilty?

Children in the nineteenth century were more often seen than heard. After a hard day's work in the cornfield under the hot summer sun, they were usually ready to retire as soon as the evening meal was over. Millard, my great-grandfather, was no exception.

Early one spring evening, as the yellow moon crept over the mountain tops, he was awakened by the rumbling of a horse-drawn wagon as it thumped over the dirt road in front of his house. He peered out the window and was astonished to see a Negro man being dragged behind an old cart. Inquisitiveness filled every fiber of his body until he could stand it no longer. He pulled on some clothes and rushed out the back door. As he tagged behind the men, he was able to pick up pieces of their conversation.

Jock, the Negro man, had been accused of raping and mutilating the body of a young white girl — a neighboring farmer's daughter. The farmer had found him standing over the body, his hands dripping with blood. Jock swore that he was innocent, but since he had worked but a short time as a hired hand, no one believed his story. He stated that he had found the girl lying between the house and the barn. Thinking that she needed help, he had stopped to give his assistance, and as he bent over the body, her father came out of the house and assumed the worst. Tempers flared, and before Jock knew what was happening, the local farmers had him convicted and on the way to the apple orchard to be hanged. No one heard his explanations as he begged for his life. The wagon was placed beneath the largest tree and a rope was knotted about his neck. As the horse pulled the wagon from beneath him, his last words rang loud and clear — "I am innocent."

Later the same spring, all but one tree in the apple orchard withered and died. Now it stands alone bearing fruit that is envied by every farmer for miles around. If one visits the orchard on the anniversary of the hanging, he can hear the faint voice of Jock calling, "I am innocent."

36: The Cooke Family

Paul and Bill Harris were riding home from church in their buggy [surrey?] and began talking of the legend of the Cooke family.

The Cookes had been pioneers and the entire family had been massacred on top of Cherry Hill on their way home from prayer meeting in 1865. It was said that the Cookes had tried again and again to reach their home over Cherry Hill.

As the Harrises were driving along, the boys noticed a man, a woman, and some children walking along the road in front of the buggy. Overtaking the family, Paul offered them a ride. The tall gentleman thanked them, and the happy group got in.

The father spoke normally of the crops, weather, and the general conditions. When they reached the top of the hill, the mother suggested that they walk from there, and, one after another, they climbed out, thanking the brothers for the ride.

As the brothers started to leave, Bill suddenly remembered that they had not asked the family's name, and he called to the little boy who was lagging behind. As he followed his family over the hill, the child replied cheerfully that his name was Jonathan Cooke.

37: The Ghosts of the Mine Horses

In the coal mines of fifty or sixty years ago, horses did much of the hauling that is now done by machinery. Each morning many horses were taken down the slope entrance into the mine, there to stand and wait until the men filled some cars with coal in the rooms. The horses would then pull the cars out of the rooms and on to the main heading. At quitting time the horses would be unharnessed and taken back out the slope and from there to the big barn that the coal company maintained. Often they would just be let loose there in the mine, and away they would go, up the slope, along the path, across the bridge, and on to the barn, unaccompanied.

When the big explosion of 1907 occurred in Old Number Six and Number Eight mines in Monongah, a great many faithful horses, as well as hundreds of brave men, perished instantly. There were eight sections in Old Number Six, and each section was approximately a mile square. In just one crosscut, in one section halfway up in Third Right of Old Number Six, at least twelve horses perished – and some said many more. These horses had been put in the crosscut to wait until the loaders filled some cars for them to pull. When the explosion came, the pressure from both ends of the crosscut pressed and squeezed the horses into one solid mass of flesh and bone.

When rescue workers could enter the mine, naturally their first concern was to locate and remove the remains

of human victims and make identification checks. This was such a tremendous and sorrowful task that at the time not too much thought was given to the bodies of the beasts of burden. When the rescue and cleanup crews came upon the big mass of twelve horses, it was decided that the best and quickest disposal that could be made was to "gob" their remains into an old working area and seal it off.

A few years after the explosion, several other men and I were working in this part of the mine where the horses had perished. Having half an hour off for lunch, we would find a place along the rib and sit on a pile of slack while we were eating. This would take about fifteen minutes; then we would have fifteen minutes to nap or, usually, just rest, before resuming work. There would then be almost complete quiet in the mine, and we would distinctly hear the galloping sound of hoofbeats. Gradually, the sounds would become louder as they approached nearer and nearer to where we were. The sounds came galloping down the heading in Third North, hoofs cracking hard on the pavement or floor of the mine, loping right upon us. We would shrink back as far as we could against the rib as the flying hoofs loped on by, the sounds finally fading in the distance.

All of us in that section heard these horses, not just once but many, many times — maybe once a week, maybe twice or three times a week, over a long period of time. None of us ever doubted that they were actual horses that galloped by, even though they were not visible to the mortal eye. We were awake and sober when we heard the sounds increasing and receding, and we knew instinctively that the clatter was made by the horses that had perished in the explosion. No man who heard the sounds could be convinced, then or now, that such things were impossible. Does one doubt the existence of the wind — be it in the form of a gentle breeze or a tornado — just because it cannot be seen by human eye?

38: The Ghost of Old Ben

Years ago seven brothers moved to Grant Town to live and earn money in the coal mines. The oldest brother was called Ben.

Ben and his brothers were very healthy, strong, and happy. They usually sat around the house after they finished working — where they ate, drank, and talked of the old country.

Ben, being the oldest, more or less took care of the younger ones. These brothers were very close to each other. They even worked in the same section together — Section Eight Main. As time passed, most of them married and had children, but they were still very close and all lived in Grant Town.

During this time, one had to be extra careful in the mines, since there were many accidents and deaths. The men had to carry lamps instead of having lights on their caps as they do today.

One day upon entering the section, Ben tripped over an old log and was killed instantly. The others felt somewhat lost without their oldest brother, but they had to go on living and taking care of their families.

One year after Ben's death, the brothers were working near Section Eight Main. Suddenly a big gust of wind came and blew out their lamps. There they stood in complete darkness, not knowing what had happened. At that moment the youngest one heard something and told the others to listen carefully. When they heard the noise – a big rumble from above – they all hit the ground and covered their heads with their arms. Then suddenly there was a cave-in.

A few seconds later they stood up and tried to feel their way around, but they could find no exit. They were sealed in to spend the last moments of their lives. All at once one of them saw a light on his left which seemed to be off in the far distance, and he pointed it out to the others. Soon the light took the form of their oldest brother, Ben, and they heard a weird voice calling, "Follow me, brothers, follow me."

The six brothers followed Old Ben until they came to another section, where men were gathered in astonishment. These men said that it was impossible for anyone to have escaped from the section where the brothers had been working.

The brothers told them of Old Ben's ghost leading them through the tunnel since they had no lights, but when they took the other men to this tunnel, the exit was sealed completely by the cave-in.

39: Friends to the End

John Boyer and Ted Klara had grown up next door to each other. Two closer friends couldn't be found. They walked to school together every morning and home together every afternoon. When someone picked on one, he was sure to hear from the other. They were also hired together in the coal mines the same day and worked side by side. Three years later Ted got married.

John felt that their life-long togetherness would be broken now that Ted was married, but it wasn't so. Nearly every night of the week, he would be over at Ted's place playing cards with the couple. The whole town was shocked when Ted and John had a falling out — evidently over Ted's wife. Ted accused John of seeing her when he wasn't around.

Even though they weren't speaking to each other, they still worked side by side in the mines. One cold February evening, while working together as usual, their silence was broken by bitter words. John told Ted he wasn't going to work with a jealous fool. When he started to walk out of the mines, he heard a loud rumble and turned just in time to see the roof falling on Ted. As he hurried back to help, a piece of slate fell on him, pinning his chest to the ground, but Ted rushed over and was able to lift it off.

John still couldn't move because his ribs were crushed. He remained there in agony until some other miners came to rescue him. When he told them what had happened, all the miners turned to one another in amazement. They knew Ted was lying dead under thirty tons of rock and couldn't have pulled the slate off John.

40: The Invisible Friend

Charles Peterman had worked for ten years in the mines and had never had an accident. During his early mining days, he had worked with Joseph Stonsin for nine weeks and in that time they had become good friends.

One day while Charles and Joseph were working deep in the mines, they heard a cracking sound, as if the timbers were breaking. Then the place started to fall in on the workers. In a quick decision, Joseph grabbed the nearest timber and held onto it to keep it from falling. In doing this he enabled Charles to escape. Two days later they found the body of Joseph Stonsin. He had been crushed by the mine fall.

After that accident Charles had been in numerous mine falls, but he had never been hurt by any of them. One time the timbers right above his head began to fall, but as if by a miracle they stopped in midair until he was clear of the danger.

When Charles was asked why the timbers had stopped and had not fallen on him, he replied, "I could see Joseph holding them and motioning me toward safety." The workers could not believe this, but then one day the same thing happened again.

No matter what Charles did or what kind of danger prevailed, he was never hurt or even scratched. Every time the workers saw Charles "saved," they asked him how he had done it. He would always say that he could see Joseph holding up the supports to save his life.

Charles finally retired from the mines, but to this day the story still goes that a ghost saved his life numerous times.

41: Eighty Feet Deep

In the days when mining first began, a man would have to work fourteen hours a day in order to feed his family. After a week of such long hard labor, on Saturday nights most of the single men would go to town to visit the local saloon.

Fred Vincent went to town one Saturday night not to go to the saloon but to get groceries for the following week. He had had an argument over a saloon girl that day with a fellow worker, and to keep out of trouble, he felt he should get his shopping done as quickly as possible and return home. As he was coming out of the store, he heard someone call his name from the shadows. He walked slowly to the corner of the building and saw Bill Sloan, the man with whom he had argued earlier that day.

Suddenly, like a bull charging toward red, Sloan lunged with full force, a shiny blade in his hand. Fred tried to disarm his attacker, but as he did so the knife slipped, and Sloan slowly fell to the ground — his face filled with hate and pain. In his last moments of life he told Fred, "You'll never be able to forget me! I'll see to that!"

Fred panicked. Since he and Bill had argued that day, he was afraid no one would believe that Sloan had called him to the shadows and that his death was accidental. He picked up the limp body and carried it to a mine shaft that had been closed down because of its danger. After placing the body several hundred yards back in the mine, he loosened a prop and ran — leaving only in time to see the entire mine collapse.

84

Two weeks later, when everyone had given up the search for the lost miner, Fred felt that the matter was closed.

One brisk fall evening as Fred was coming home from the mines, he heard someone call his name. Then he heard the sentence, "I'll never let you forget." His blood chilled and he stopped still. But only the leaves falling slowly, softly, gently to the ground made another sound. He walked to his cabin in silence, wondering who or what he had heard.

About two months had gone by and Fred kept thinking of Sloan's dying words. One night at about 8:30, he seemed particularly restless as he worked in the mine — perhaps because they were deeper into the mine than they had ever gone.

Suddenly his lamp went out, and as it did, another one lit beyond him. But how could that be? No one had ever been any farther than he. Nothing was there but rock.

Fred felt a breeze and at the same moment a man spoke his name. He turned to run and saw that the men behind him had gone home for the night. He then saw a man who looked like Bill Sloan. The man walked up to him, and Fred saw that a knife was sticking in his stomach. The man *was* Bill Sloan — and he said, "You'll never forget me!"

When the men returned the next day, they found Fred with a piece of glass in his stomach and his shattered lamp lying beside him. They felt that his death was accidental. But was it?

42: The Swinging Lantern

During the early 1850s when the railroads were coming into North Carolina, a strange event occurred which has never been fully explained. A conductor on a Southern Railroad express train was signaling for the engineer to start the train, when, as it began to move, he slipped and fell to the tracks. He was killed instantly, of course.

The next day the conductor's body was buried without his head, for it had been cut off by the train wheels and could not be found. The head was *never* found, and the incident was finally forgotten.

Months later, the ghost of the conductor reappeared. Night after night, the citizens of Wrightsville saw a lantern, or at least what appeared to be a lantern, swinging from side to side as it came down the tracks. The people demanded an explanation of this strange phenomenon, and the mayor summoned several experts from all over the United States.

This group of scientists stayed at a site beside the tracks for three days, waiting for the lantern to appear. They were about to give up when finally the light came swinging down the tracks within about three yards of the men and suddenly darted toward the woods.

The next morning the scientists wrote up individual reports. The final conclusion was drawn up and published in the Wrightsville Beach newspaper: "This swinging light defies all the scientific knowledge of our time and it cannot be said that the light does not exist."

To the people of Wrightsville there is only one explanation possible. The conductor, who was buried over a hundred years ago, is still searching for his head and carries the same lantern he used on the old Southern express.

43: Van Meter's Plight

George Van Meter's small farm was in Dorcas Hollow, just five miles south of the present site of Petersburg, West Virginia. George was a carpenter from Germany. He had settled with his family at Dorcas when there were only fifteen families in the whole county. At that time the Huron Indians were rampaging throughout the whole valley. Some of the early settlers had already been killed in Indian raids. George was one of the many isolated farmers whose cabins were a good way from the settlement.

On the morning of July 4, while most of the settlement was preparing for the coming celebration, George Van Meter was in a small field near his cabin. His son was helping him while the rest of the family was getting ready to leave for the big day at the settlement.

George and young David had just stopped for a much needed rest when a small band of Indians came running out of the woods across the field. The father told his son to run for the cabin and take the others to the settlement. He would try to fight off the band long enough for the boy to get the family to safety. That was the last time any of George's family was to see him alive.

Young David Van Meter made it to the settlement with

the rest of the family and warned the town folk. A group of men, accompanied by David, left to rescue George. When they reached the farm, a sickening sight met their eyes. The ox George was plowing with had been killed, and the cabin had been burned to the ground. Only the chimneys that had stood at each end of the cabin were left.

George's body was found a few feet from the cabin he had given his life for. His head had been completely severed from his body. Although the men searched the farm the rest of the day and into the night, they did not find the head. The next day the whole settlement prepared for an Indian attack.

The Indians never showed up at the settlement, but George Van Meter's head did. On the day after the raid, a small boy found a cooking pot on the steps of the meetinghouse cabin. When the pot was opened before the settlers' eyes, George's face was staring at them. The Indians had boiled his head in the pot — a most horrifying sight to behold.

For years after the event, no one would go near the Van Meter place. There was a reason for this: some people said that on several occasions a headless body had been seen wandering about the old ruins as if it were searching for something. Was it possible that George could have been coming back, searching for his ill-fated head?

Today the two chimneys can still be seen from Route 28, out of Petersburg. Most people pass the site, never realizing the story that lies behind those chimneys.

44: The Old Man's Reward

One night an old man went to a farmer's house and asked to stay there overnight. He was told he could sleep there, provided he would go out to the little haunted house in the backyard. The farmer promised to give him a bag of money if he would stay in the little house until morning.

The stranger went to the house and got ready for bed, but before retiring he sat on the floor and began reading his Bible. He heard something rolling and went out to investigate, but found nothing. He began reading again and heard something skating. He investigated again, but found nothing. These noises went on until early in the morning. A knock sounded on the old man's door, and on opening it, he found a headless man standing there with a hatchet in his hand.

The headless man took him by the hand, led him down the stairs to a little door at the end of the hall. He took the hatchet, knocked the door in, pulled out a bag of money, and handed it to the stranger. Then he disappeared. The old man had received his reward for staying all night in the old Simpson place.

45: The Headless Man

Many years ago the people of a certain town had to pass a cemetery on their way to a little church up on the hill. Several people told of seeing a headless man who appeared in the distance before them. No one had had the courage to speak to the man — to ask him why he was there or what he wanted.

At dusk one evening a young man was passing the cemetery and suddenly the headless man appeared in front of him. Although he was startled by the appearance of such a thing, the young man got up enough courage to speak. He asked him why he was there and what he wanted. After hearing the reply to his questions, the horrified young man went on home.

The next day, some of the townspeople who had heard of the episode went to the young man's house to find out what the headless man had said to him. After they knocked several times, the young man appeared at the door.

The townspeople looked at him with astonishment. He no longer appeared young and handsome as he had before. His hair was white, his skin looked old and wrinkled, and there was a strange glassy look in his eyes.

When the townspeople asked him what had happened, he only nodded his head and went back into the house, closing the door behind him. No one ever found out what the headless man said to him.

46: Dog Rock

Clem Robinson lived at the head of Robinson Hollow, which was named after him. He was a man with a very violent temper. It is said that when he became angry at something, he would beat it to death or tear it apart, no matter what it might be. So it was with one of his foxhounds.

One night Clem was fox hunting in Robinson Hollow, and one of his hounds scented a rabbit's trail and began to follow it. As the dog chased the rabbit, Clem became very angry. He tried to call the dog back, but it paid no attention to him. This enraged him, and when the dog did return to him, he was so angry that he picked up a log and beat the animal's head off. After he had done this to the dog, it ran and rolled down the hill and into the creek.

The creek is lined on both sides by very steep and rocky hills. It has been told that at night people have seen a headless dog running down one side of the hill, across the creek, and up the other side of the hill. Clem also saw the headless ghost of his foxhound as he returned home one night. After seeing the ghost of his dog, he changed his ways and did not show such brutality toward his animals.

47: The Headless Dog of Tug Fork

A schoolhouse used to stand on a little rise near the road leading from Mill Creek to Tug Fork. The house had been gone for many years when people living in the settlement near there began to speak of seeing the headless dog that came out of the heap of stones on the site of the old chimney.

The cause of the ghost dog's appearance there has never been explained. Some people hint that long ago when the country was thinly settled and people were not very inquisitive concerning one another's doings, a traveler and his dog were killed by robbers and buried under the schoolhouse.

There are several persons living in Mill Creek who remember hearing reliable people tell of seeing the spectral dog — and even of being followed by it.

One man was traveling the road on horseback after dark. Just as he rounded the bend where the old schoolhouse had stood, he plainly saw by the light of the full moon a large black dog coming down the bank from the chimney place. It came into the road and followed him. Having heard of the creature before, the traveler put spurs to his horse and rode rapidly away from the gloomy place, but the dog bounded after him swiftly, and actually leaped on the horse's back behind the frightened man. Casting a glance backward, he saw the ghastly creature sitting calmly behind him, its bloody neck from which the head was missing almost touching him. The horse apparently was not aware of the horrid spectre, but the man certainly was — although he dared not look behind him the second time until he had reached a settlement several miles away, whereupon he found the dog had vanished.

One night nearly thirty years ago, three young men were walking home from a meeting on Tug Fork. Their way homeward led past the haunted house site. Probably they had all heard tales about the headless dog and regarded them as made-up stories. They passed the heap of stones on the rise above the road, where they saw nothing unusual by the light of the brightly shining moon. But some distance beyond there one of the young fellows looked back and noticed a large black dog following closely behind them.

He called the attention of the others to the animal and they stopped to observe it more closely; their observation convinced them that it was the headless dog and that it cast no shadow on the ground where it walked in the bright moonlight. Without saying much, the young men traveled as rapidly as possible the rest of the way home, but the dog still followed them and even went ahead, gamboling and rolling at their feet. One youth struck at it with a cane, but the cane went through the spectre as though it were a shadow — and stuck in the road. After this the young men broke into a run, the dog keeping close to them until they reached a creek.

Here the dog turned back, evidently very reluctant to do so, as it could be seen in the moonlight to stop now and then and turn in the direction of the terrified youths, who lost no time in widening the distance between themselves and the horrible spectre.

48: The Legend of the Haunted House

On a hill in Harrison County stands an old abandoned house. It is a pretty, white house, with a large yard, and in the summer it is surrounded by many kinds of flowers. This house has been empty for a little over a year. It is not a spooky-looking place that everyone would be afraid of, but for some reason none of the families who have bought it have lived there more than a month, in spite of its beautiful location. Some people believe the house is haunted.

This legend was probably strengthened one rainy night when Lee Harris, a traveling salesman, was passing through that section. He had a flat tire just down the road from the house. Seeing a light in the window, he decided to ask the people who lived there if he could use their telephone to call a repair station.

A very beautiful woman opened the door. Her hair was golden blonde and waved down her back; her eyes were as blue as the sky on a bright spring day; indeed, the man was enchanted by her many charms. She was joined at the door by three small children, bright-eyed and much like their mother. The salesman called a repair shop and found that a bridge had been washed away, and no one could come to fix the tire until the next morning.

When Lee explained where he was, the man did not believe that a woman and three children were in the house; he told the salesman to get away from the place as soon as possible — to sleep in his car, if he had to. Lee could not understand this because the woman treated him so nicely. She offered him a cup of coffee and told him he could spend the night in her house – and he accepted her hospitality.

He had a very comfortable night until about 12:30, when he heard the children screaming. At first he thought they were having youthful nightmares and would soon go back to sleep. But the screaming persisted, and he decided the woman could use some help in getting the youngsters quieted.

When he got downstairs, he was amazed at what he saw. It was the same beautiful woman he had encountered just a few hours before, but she looked entirely different – thin, rough, and almost ugly. Her once beautiful bright eyes were darkened and glassy with a look of torture. The children, now wearing ragged clothing, were not even clean, and they were crying from hunger.

Lee spoke to the woman and asked her why she didn't feed the youngsters, but she only kept on screaming at them and begging them not to cry, as though she hadn't heard him speak to her at all. He walked over and touched her arm, trying to keep her from the children. When he touched her flesh, he found it was cold, as if in death. Could it be that all of them were dead? Lee used all his strength in trying to keep her from harming her offspring, but nothing he did seemed to stop her.

Finally she led the little ones out the back door. Lee followed them, sorry for the children and curious. He saw the woman line them up according to their ages. She took the smallest, who was about two years old, and led him by the neck to the well. Lee rushed to her but it was too late; she had murdered the little boy, once bright-eyed and happy. Lee turned to the other children but with all

95

his power he could not move them from their positions. The woman took the next child, who was about four, and proceeded to do the same with her; the five-year-old was next. After this she knelt by the well and began praying to God to look after her beautiful children. She did love them so, but she had no money and could not bear to see them tortured by starvation.

The woman then rushed into the house and cut her wrists. She died on the kitchen floor. Lee went upstairs to get a blanket to lay over her, but when he returned, the body had disappeared. He looked everywhere, but it was gone. There was only the stillness of the early morning and the sun coming through the window.

When the man from the service station finally came that morning, he was surprised to find Lee in the house. He said the house was haunted – that everyone who moved into it heard the voices of children screaming as though they were in pain. Lee asked about the lovely woman, but the repairman didn't seem to know anything about any woman living in the house with three children.

Lee did not tell the man about what he had seen, but he felt he had learned the real story behind the haunted house – and perhaps he had.

49: The Man on the Railroad

It was a cool summer night. As my great-grandfather sat on his back porch overlooking the railroad tracks, little did he know he was about to see the town ghost — the man on the railroad.

My great-grandfather had moved to Colliers, West Virginia, just two weeks before. As he sat on the back porch of his new home this particular night, he noticed an old man walking on the railroad tracks. He did not think this was strange, since hobos often waited to jump the train. But this man tonight was different.

As grandfather observed him, the hobo kept taking a drink of something out of a bottle. After a while he sat down on the tracks and kept drinking from the bottle. It was obvious that the man was drunk and soon would be insensible. If he were aware of what was going on even now, he would move away from the tracks, because the 9:15 freight train was due in five minutes. But the man sat there without moving an inch, and he continued drinking from the same bottle which, it seemed, would never run dry.

At this point my great-grandfather was getting a little worried. My great-grandmother had joined him on the porch and she too was aware of the scheduled train. She urged her husband to go and help the man.

The tracks were about a fourth of a mile from the house, and my great-grandfather started to run down in the direction of the man. He had only about four minutes to reach him.

He ran faster, and in the distance he heard the train's

warning whistle. Would he be able to reach the man in time? He told himself he had to. He began to shout, "You fool, get out of there before you're killed!" But the man paid no attention whatever to the warning.

Great-grandfather heard the train drawing nearer. He knew it would soon reach the spot where the man was sitting. Since the engine was so high, the engineer would not be able to see him and would not bring the train to a stop.

It was already too late. The train was right there, and a horrible death was about to occur before my great-grandfather's eyes. But much to his amazement, before the engine struck the man, the old hobo had disappeared into thin air!

At first my great-grandfather thought he was seeing things and waited for the train to pass to prove to himself that someone had really been sitting there. However, there was no trace of anyone. He was positive he had seen a man. His wife had seen him too, for she had suggested that he go down and help him, but now he was gone!

Great-grandfather returned home quite shaken up and told his wife what had happened although she had watched the scene herself. They both were disturbed over the matter and decided to keep it a secret. After about a week the mystery troubled them so much that they told their landlord about the strange night.

Expecting to be called silly or crazy as they revealed their story, they were surprised when the landlord instead listened intently, with a serious look on his face.

When my great-grandfather finished his story, the land-lord began to explain what the two had seen.

A long time before, an old man whom no one had ever seen before appeared in the town. Being wary of strangers, the people refused to give him food, shelter, or even a job. The stranger got drunk, and for the good of the town he was driven away.

The only thing the stranger knew how to do was jump trains, and so he sat down on the tracks waiting for the next freight. When the train came, the man on the railroad was mangled to pieces.

Every year at the time of his death, this man would return and wait for the train. Whenever people would try to ride past the tracks on the anniversary of his death, the horses would buck and would go no farther. No one had ever succeeded in getting past the tracks on this particular date. My great-grandfather was the only one ever to go near them on that strange night. He thought he saw a man in trouble and tried to help him.

A year after the incident, my great-grandfather waited to see the man on the railroad appear again. It was 9:10 — five more minutes and the train would pass. There was no sign of the hobo. At last the train passed and no man appeared.

No one has seen the man on the railroad since. Some people believe that great-grandfather satisfied what the ghost had waited for all these years — a person with a human heart to help someone in need.

50: The Girl in the Green Coat

Driving home one afternoon, a man saw a little girl suddenly appear in front of his car. He slammed on his brakes and turned the steering wheel, trying to miss the child, but it was too late. He could feel a thump against the car as it hit her body.

The frightened man ran to a nearby house. After he had knocked several times, a woman finally appeared. He told her that he had just hit a little girl and asked if he could use her telephone to call an ambulance.

The woman asked him if the girl was wearing a green coat and a red scarf. The man nodded. He would not need to call an ambulance, the woman said. The child was her little girl, but she had been dead over five years. Her daughter had been hit by a car at the very spot on which his car was sitting, and she had been wearing a green coat and red scarf at the time. The man looked at her in astonishment.

The woman went on to explain that several times before someone had been driving along and suddenly seen a little girl, wearing a green coat and a red scarf, jump in front of the car.

Hardly able to believe the story, the man walked back to his car. When he looked at the road in front of his car, the girl was gone.

51: The Blue Gown

Many years ago, in the vicinity of Clarksburg, a young lad of twelve had to run an errand late at night. The family lived in a large two-story house on top of a hill that sloped down to a gully leading to the river, which was about half a mile away.

As the boy was hurrying home that cold November evening, something caught his eye. There, in the freezing temperature, a woman went walking by him. She was dressed in a blue evening gown of flowing chiffon, and she didn't seem to notice either the boy or the cold.

She was walking down the hill, and the boy decided to follow her. He called out to her several times, but she did not seem to hear; she just kept on walking, her gown flowing in the brisk air. He noticed that she was barefooted, in spite of the cold night and the evening dress she wore.

The boy followed her along the gully that led straight to the river. Finally she came to the river's edge, and without stopping she gently walked into the icy water until she disappeared. He waited for her to return, but she did not. After waiting for what seemed an hour, he couldn't stand the cold any longer and went back home. He tried to sleep, but couldn't stop thinking about what had happened.

He told his family about it the next day, but no one believed him. After everyone had half-convinced him that he must have been dreaming or sleepwalking, his little brother came running into the house with a piece of blue chiffon he had found on the path the boy had taken the night before.

52: Returning Suicide

In the 1920s there was an old white house near Monongah that was said to be haunted. It was a large house, and a woman in white was supposed to have jumped to her death from a window of one of the upstairs bedrooms.

Faith Harris was a young woman when her family bought the house and moved in against the warnings of the people who lived nearby. They said no one had been able to live in the house any length of time since the woman's death, and the last family who lived there had moved out after only a week.

Since the suicide, no one had slept in the room from which the woman had leaped, but it was said that she haunted that part of the house and made nightly visits there. People claimed to have seen her walking the grounds in her white dress.

Faith wouldn't believe such stories and took the bedroom as her own. Preparing for bed the first night she raised the window, and as she did, she saw a white figure walking slowly up the path towards the house. She laughed to herself, thinking it must be one of the family coming home, and went to bed.

The next morning when she did not come downstairs for breakfast, and everyone had called her several times, her sister went up to get her. When she entered the room, there was Faith, lying half on and half off the bed, her face beaten black and blue, and her body bruised all over. The room was a shambles.

When she was able to talk, Faith told of the voice she had heard as she lay between sleeping and waking the night before. Someone was shaking her and saying, "Get up! Get out! Here, take it; it's money!"

Thinking it was one of her sisters playing a practical joke, she sleepily pushed the hands away and said, "Oh, get away and let me sleep!"

And the next thing she knew, she felt a terrible pain, and then another, on her face again and again, until nothing seemed to matter except sleep and unconsciousness.

53: The Old Gray Mare Conquers the Unknown

Block Stanley was as sturdy a man as his name implied. He built his life on the motto that all work and no play was the only way to build a good farm. His one weakness was the love of coon hunting. His greatest pleasure was to take his mare Old Nellie and his dogs out at night to tree a coon. No one else would take a horse on a coon hunt, but Block was by no means an ordinary man.

One night in the late fall, when the bare trees lifted their black branches toward the yellow moon, he decided to join a few neighbors in their favorite pastime. Joined in the companionship of drink and good humor, they sat around the campfire until dawn. As the first light of dawn crept over the hill, the dogs jumped a coon. They cornered it in the field adjoining the Madison graveyard. The condition of this field had long aroused speculation:

103

no one grazed cattle or mowed the field, and yet it was always green and looked as if the grass had been freshly cut. Although Block was aware of certain tales about the field told by the superstitious townspeople, he disregarded them with the aplomb of an individualist. He was convinced that there was some logical explanation. While the others stood in indecision, Block went into the field after the coon.

Suddenly the men heard a scream and observed Block suspended in the air without visible means of support. As immobile as statues, the men remained in fixed positions, and Block called to his old mare for help. The horse that he had left standing nearby went to him without hesitation. Grabbing hold of the saddle, he ordered her to get him out of that field. It was as if dozens of people were holding him back; the mare pulled with all her might and yet was barely able to move him. Finally, after struggling for about two hundred feet, Block suddenly dropped to the ground. He lay prone, as a cold breeze rippled through the tattered shreds of his shirt and trousers.

The stunned and speechless men helped him back to the flickering fire. Afraid to venture forth without the safety of daylight, they sat until the pink dawn erased all shadows. Looking for an explanation, the men went into the field to see if there had been barbed wire that could have grabbed or held him in such a manner, but there was absolutely nothing. Block swore that something or someone had tried to pull him into the great unknown.

Needless to say, he never went hunting near the cemetery again.

54: The Haunted House of Shell Creek

In Maryland, near Shell Creek, there is a very mysterious house. This old yellow-brick structure is supposed to have been a slave jail at one time; in the cellar there are cells, some of which still enclose the remains of former inhabitants. People living nearby have heard mournful cries, and some have claimed to have heard chains rattling and to have seen lights in the house at various times. But these unusual happenings are not the only haunts of the house. There is one more.

During the 1800s a very wealthy southern gentleman bought the house. He had a lovely daughter and had arranged for her to marry into an equally wealthy family upon her eighteenth birthday.

By her eighteenth birthday, however, she had met and fallen in love with a young man from a comparatively poor family. Her father was so upset by this that he sealed her in a cell he had built in the wall. She had with her a red handkerchief her lover had given her, and she is supposed to have died clutching it in her hand.

Every night at midnight she walks, looking for her lost love. She walks along the bank of the creek and at one point drops her handkerchief, which is to be picked up by her lover.

One evening a young girl happened to be passing the house shortly after midnight when the figure of a lady caught her eye. The woman wore a long white gown and carried in her hand a red handkerchief. As she walked along, the handkerchief dropped from her hand.

The young girl picked it up to give to the owner, but the handkerchief vanished, right in her hand, and as she turned toward the lady, she disappeared also.

55: The Light in Mother's Room

On the bank of Little Buffalo Creek near Rowlesburg was a small farm belonging to a widow named Sanders. She had four grown sons who had land and families of their own.

Old Mrs. Sanders died in 1927, and according to some of the neighbors, her will provided that her goods should be divided equally among her four sons. But her sons could not agree on the exact division of the property.

One night when the argument was especially violent, the youngest, Dave, noticed a strange light coming from the upper hall. He immediately went upstairs to investigate. Upon entering the hall, he found that the light was coming from his mother's room. When he pushed open the door, the corner where his mother's rocking chair stood was flooded with a bright vibrating light. His cries brought his brothers to the room, stopping the argument, and as they watched in silence, the light slowly faded.

The next night the argument started again, and as before, the strange light came pouring down the stairs.

106

The brothers decided that it must be reflecting from something outside. They turned off all the lights and rushed out of the house to see, but the night was starless and pitch black; there was not a thing that could cause a reflection. As the brothers watched from outside, the light slowly dimmed and vanished.

On two more occasions when the Sanders brothers met to "discuss" their mother's will, the light appeared. The last time, they became brave enough to poke the offending corner with a broomstick, and then with their hands. But nothing was there.

Dave Sanders told his brothers that the light was caused by their consciences, and they decided he was right. They knew they were behaving badly by arguing, and they thought that they had all imagined the light.

But that explanation was shattered the next day when a neighbor stopped in for coffee and asked the brothers why they burned so many lights in their mother's room at night. He said he could see the light from his cabin, and it looked almost as if the room was on fire.

The will was settled quickly and quietly, in the way the boys thought would have made their mother happy. The strange, vibrating light was never seen again.

56: The Lynchers

Many years ago, around the turn of the century, there lived in the easternmost part of Taylor County a bachelor who operated what was then considered a very large orchard. (Evidently it wasn't the size of orchards we know today, for he was the sole worker.) The townsfolk were all leery of the old gentleman and would never venture near his farm. All the apples he sold were carted into town — by him.

One fall a new family moved into the area and bought a farm adjoining the old bachelor's property. There was a little boy in the family, and one evening he climbed over the fence and sneaked into the orchard. Like most boys he was quite active, and he began to climb the trees and run and play — until he noticed the old man coming toward him. Not knowing what the townsfolk suspected, he approached the man and started to talk to him.

The old man turned out to be quite friendly, and the two became close friends as time went on.

One day as the boy played in the old man's trees he fell to the ground and died instantly from a broken neck. When the townsfolk found how the boy had died, they immediately suspected the old man of foul play. A lynching party composed of nine men was organized, and they hanged the old man from one of the apple trees in his orchard.

That winter a terrible freeze killed every tree in the entire orchard except the one on which the old man had been hanged. It developed into one of the most bountiful fruit bearers ever seen in the area. This lone tree bore as many apples as all the other trees had, put together. The orchard was sold to another farmer, who harvested the apples and sold them in the nearby community.

Eight of the men who had composed the lynching party were among the buyers. These eight died very mysteriously and unexpectedly. Later on, investigation showed that they had all eaten fruit from the old man's tree. It seemed quite strange, since no one else was poisoned.

The ninth man had refused to eat the apples. He thought he had broken the curse.

The following spring another tree in the orchard came to life and began to turn green with leaves. It looked as though it would also bear fruit. The ninth man from the lynching party happened to be going along the road by the farm. When he saw another tree bearing a lone apple, he got off his horse and picked it.

It had been so long since he had eaten an apple that he couldn't help being tempted to taste it. He died when his teeth pierced the skin.

Neither tree bore fruit again. It appears that they had completed their task, though they continued to live on for years. One was the tree from which the old man was hanged; the other, the tree from which the boy fell to his death.

57: The Cline House

The Cline house was an old farmhouse on Lost River, about two miles outside of Mathias, West Virginia. A peddler was killed in one of the upstairs bedrooms of the place, and people were afraid to move in afterwards because the peddler had said with his dying breath that he would come back and kill anyone who lived there.

The house had long been labeled a haunted house when John and Mary Smith moved into it on the first day of summer. One morning, about a week after the Smiths had moved into the house, Mary was sitting on the porch with a basket of eggs she had just gathered when she heard a strange noise at the upstairs window. It was a weird, sniffing noise, and when she looked at the window she didn't see anyone or anything that could have caused it. This puzzled her, but she soon forgot it.

That night after Mary and John went to bed there were noises in the next room. Someone or something that had been feeling along the wall and moaning suddenly fell to the floor with a loud scream. John got out of bed and ran into the next room. At first glance, the room seemed completely empty, but when he took a second look, he noticed there was something red on the floor and several large claw marks down the wall. He stood there startled, because this was the room in which the peddler was murdered. He decided not to tell Mary anything about it, since she had slept through it all, and he went back to bed.

There was a staircase that ran from the room in which the peddler was killed down to the porch. The door at the bottom of this staircase opened onto the porch, but it could never be kept closed. The Smiths tried locking it and just about every other means of keeping it shut, but nothing worked. Finally they nailed it shut.

John and Mary were eating supper out on the porch one warm evening, when all of a sudden they heard something come rolling down the steps. All the nails popped out of the door and a large burlap bag rolled out on the floor and then disappeared.

John told his neighbors about this, and they told him the story of how the murderers dumped the peddler into a large burlap bag and tried to bury the body before someone found it. They warned him to move out of the house as soon as possible, but he decided to stay as long as nothing else happened.

Sometime later a couple of the Smiths' neighbors went to check on them, since they hadn't heard from them for two weeks. When they arrived at the house, the first thing they noticed was that three burlap bags were lying on the porch. One was empty, but the other two had something in them. When they looked into the two full bags, they were shocked to find the dead bodies of Mary and John, cut up and stuffed into the bags.

No one else ever occupied the house again because it burned to the ground a few days later.

58: The Seated Lady

A favorite tale of the old people in Jane Lew, West Virginia, had its setting in a long-forgotten cemetery in the area. Among the gravestones there had been a remarkable one of marble – a statue of a seated lady with outstretched hands. The woman for whom the statue had been erected had died of a broken heart when her fiancé married another woman.

Years later, the young people of the community started a club. As new members joined the organization, an initiation was required. Each new member had to spend one night sitting in the statue's lap.

All went well until one very dark, moonless night. At the appointed time, a young girl stole from her home and hastened to the cemetery. There she cautiously made her way through the tombstones to the seated lady. Trembling, she sat in the marble lap. Although she did not know it, this girl had more reason to be frightened than others. She happened to be a direct descendant of the traitorous fiancé.

The citizens of the community did not sleep well that night. Something kept their nerves on edge. They did not know what they feared.

The next morning the young girl was discovered, still sitting in the statue's lap. She was dead. On her body were found marks as though she had been held in a superhuman clinch. Perhaps the seated lady had gained revenge.

59: The Power of Love

Darkness was setting in early, for winter was just around the corner. The huge oak trees surrounding the old grave-yard were starting to lose their leaves and the late autumn wind had a crisp tingle in it. The full moon was bright yellow as old J. W. Collins looked through the hazy mist into the dark sky. He puffed on his short, briar pipe and slowly made his nightly rounds of the cemetery as he had done for several years. Just as he was returning from checking the lock on the north gate he noticed two moving shadows, which gradually formed into a strolling young couple as they approached.

Old J. W. smiled and said, "Sorry, but I just finished locking the north gate. You will have to use the south entrance. You folks startled me there at first. I'm not used to running into people up here. Not too many couples pick this place to go for a walk, you know."

Neither of the handsome young people replied, but the tall man smiled as they turned toward the south gate. J. W. stood with his eyes following the stranger's white raincoat until he and his companion disappeared into the darkness.

Old J. W. let the mysterious couple fade from his mind as he continued on his rounds, the smoke puffing from the bowl of his pipe. He pulled his worn, brown coat tighter around his body as the wind picked up and the fog began to set in. Finally he completed his nightly task and was about to retire to his small shack in the rear of the cemetery when he heard several loud noises.

An old car rattled to a screeching stop and two men

leaped from it, calling to J. W. when they saw the beam from his flashlight. He admitted the breathless pair through the south gate and listened to their excited babbling.

The two men were Dr. Harold Johnson and George Ellis. They were desperately searching for George's brother, Ralph, who had that night escaped from their guardian custody. Ralph's young wife, Gloria, had recently died, and he was insane with grief. The doctor and George thought that there was a good chance Ralph might return to his wife's grave. The two worried men asked J. W. to lead them to the week-old grave of Gloria Ellis. When the trio approached the spot, J. W. suddenly stopped and exclaimed, "Look, the grave has been opened!"

Dr. Johnson spoke quickly as he looked at George, then back to J. W. "The poor, deranged fellow. He must have taken her out of here! J. W., have you noticed anyone in the graveyard tonight? Ralph is tall and he is wearing a white raincoat."

Old J. W. stood for a long moment and listened to the whistling of the wind before he made an attempt to answer. Finally, he looked solemnly into the doctor's eyes and said, "Sorry, Doc, but I haven't seen anyone tonight. No sir, no one at all."

60: Death of a Minister's Wife

The room was very dark and quiet. Four tiny candles spread a soft glow over the face of the figure in the bed. If one looked closely, he could see that the features were those of a woman. She was rather heavily built, but she had carried her weight with grace and beauty. Her face was not wrinkled, except for small raylike lines at the outer corners of her mouth and eyes.

This lady was my great-grandmother. She was in terrible pain, and the doctor was expected to arrive at any moment. Her husband, John, was a Methodist minister and had been at her side all that day and all the previous night. The end seemed to be near.

At that moment the family doctor entered the room. He said a few words of comfort to Grandpa John and went over to attend great-grandma.

She was having a difficult time breathing. Her breath came in hard, struggling gasps. She half rose from her pillow, clutched at her throat, and within seconds was dead. The doctor tried everything, but all efforts to revive her failed. Great-grandma was pronounced dead of a heart attack.

Grandpa John knelt by her bed and began praying, while the doctor left the room to gather the four children. Bruce, the oldest, had been his mother's favorite, and grandpa knew that her death would be especially hard on him.

The four children came into the room, their eyes puffy

and streaming with tears. All of them became hysterical and had to be taken from the room except Bruce. He stared at his mother in disbelief and anguish. He asked that he be left alone with her for a while and grandpa went out of the room.

Suddenly Bruce fell to his knees beside the bed. He cried and prayed with all his heart. He said only one sentence over and over again, as he hugged her and tried to pull her into a sitting position on the bed. He sobbed, "Mamma, come back — I need you!"

All of a sudden, his mother's eyelids began to flutter slightly. Then her eyes opened and she caught her breath. Before the boy's staring eyes, she spoke. "Bruce, is that you? Don't cry, dear. Mamma's here now."

Bruce called out frantically to the others who came running into the room. None of the family could believe it; they were numb with fear and disbelief. To think that they could have buried her alive!

When everyone had calmed down a little, great-grandma asked them all to be quiet. She had something important to tell them. "Children and family, I know that what I am going to tell you will seem unbelievable, but I must tell you anyway. I saw heaven! I remember gasping for breath and from the pain that seemed to smother my heart.

"In a moment the pain was gone. I seemed to be floating away from my body out into darkness. In the distance, I saw the most beautiful glow I have ever seen anywhere — huge, transparent buildings bathed in a golden light, fountains in the air, soft green grass, and flowers — all in a spacious garden.

"But just as I was about to place my foot upon that grass, something strange happened. I heard a tiny, piti-

116

ful, childish voice coming up to me in the darkness. I began to fall — down, down, down. I knew the voice was Bruce's. No mother could go away, even to God's house, when her son cries out to her in that utterly wretched voice, "Mamma, come back — I need you!"

61: Lamented Love

Early in the nineteenth century in Wayne County, West Virginia, there was a young boy, Josh, and a young girl, Holly, who were very much in love. However, their families were bitter enemies. In order to escape the wrath and disapproval of their parents, they met in a wooded area that was parklike in appearance. Beautiful flowers appeared from nowhere in this remote place, and holly grew in abundance. It was as if God had created it especially for these two young lovers.

During their courtship, the young girl became heavy with child. It was not long before her father learned of his daughter's deception. Even though she was to be a mother, he refused to let her marry the young man.

Determined that she should not bear an illegitimate child, Josh and Holly planned to elope and be married. Hearing of their plans, the father followed Holly to the secret meeting place and found the two together. He shot Josh through the heart, killing him instantly. The girl went into a state of shock and wandered about in a daze. Life without Josh was not worth living. The following day she returned to the same spot and committed suicide.

The legend continues that all the holly and beautiful flowers died; the ground cracked, and for a year not a blade of grass grew in this secluded place. The following spring, two weeping willow trees appeared on the very spot where the two had died. Rippling springs emerged beneath the trees, and grass sprang from the scorched earth. On the anniversary of their death, they can be seen searching for each other. Josh can be heard calling for Holly, while she sits beneath the willow tree, weeping for her lost love.

62: The Rosebush

Many, many years ago, on the outskirts of Grafton, there lived a very rich family for those times by the name of Allts. There were only three of them — Mr. and Mrs. Jim Allts and their daughter, Anna. They seemed to be blessed with everything except health for the daughter. Mr. and Mrs. Allts took her to every doctor, far and near, but no cure could be found for her illness.

One cold, wintry night in early December, the girl seemed to make a sudden recovery. She even got up out of bed and walked that night, and this was something she had never been able to do. But now the girl seemed to be a different person — she was in some kind of trance. As she got up from her bed, she walked to the door and went out onto the new-fallen snow. She walked down through the yard and out to a rosebush she had always admired from her window in the spring and summer.

Suddenly, she collapsed beside it and died, with her hands resting near the base of the bush. From that time on, the rosebush bloomed the year round. Even in midwinter you could see beautiful red roses peeping through the snow.

Several years later the Allts family moved from the house and decided to take the rosebush with them, because it had been so dear to their daughter. They planted the bush in their new yard, but it failed to bloom that spring or summer. The Allts feared it had died.

That very December, on the anniversary of their daughter's death, there was a light sifting snow that covered the ground. When Mr. and Mrs. Allts awoke the next morning, the rosebush had disappeared, and footprints led away from the spot where it had stood.

The footprints led straight to the cemetery and stopped right in front of their daughter's grave. There on the grave stood the rosebush, its red roses looking more beautiful than ever!

63: The Dead Girl Revived

Jane Reynolds was in her teens when her health began to fail. As time passed she grew worse, and, over a period of years, she weakened until she was completely bedfast. Her family took her to doctors all over the country, but nothing seemed to help. Finally she became so weak that she could not even feed herself.

Through it all, she remained kind and gentle, with a

cheerful disposition, even though she realized she had only a short time to live. One day a very close friend came to see her and sat with her a while. Although Jane was too weak to talk, her friend, who was very religious, sat beside her four hours and held her hand.

Sometime later, as other members of the family came into the room, the girl by the bedside suddenly knew that her friend was gone. But she continued to sit and hold her hand.

Two of the family members, realizing the situation, urged her to come away, but she said, "I can't." On further questioning, she said, "I *cannot* let loose of her hand."

They were all so shocked and upset by this that considerable time passed before they called in the family physician and other members of the family to verify the fact that Jane was really dead. Still the friend could not free her hand. But she was very calm and peaceful through it all, in spite of the agitated feelings of the family, and continued to sit there hour after hour, with a quiet faith.

Suddenly the girl who had been pronounced dead several hours before came to life. She opened her eyes, and at the instant she did, the friend was able to release her hand.

Jane very quietly told the members of her family that everything was all right — that she had had an unbelievably beautiful experience. She could not tell them about it then, but would in time. She said she felt extremely well, but would like them to leave the room. She asked that they go down and prepare dinner. She wanted to take a bath, which she hadn't been able to do by herself for years, and afterwards she would come down too.

The family were astounded by all this, and it took them some time to come to believe that she had had a full and complete recovery.

Some years later, the girl, having been deeply moved by her experience with death and her very evident glimpse into the afterlife, decided to go into the ministry, and it is said that those who heard her preach were deeply impressed by her sincerity.

64: Twice Twins

Mrs. Adams sat by the fireside dreaming in a lonely way about the wonderful times of the past with her beloved husband, Edwin. She had been so terribly lonely since his death that she spent many sleepless nights before the fireplace hopelessly longing for his return. Her melancholy world was based solely on his memory. She sadly regretted that she had been the only one at his quiet funeral. Even his only brother, his twin, Ronald, had died shortly before Edwin had his unexpected heart attack.

Although it was apparent that Ronald had been inferior and a discredit to the family, she could not understand Edwin's contempt, hatefulness, and overbearing attitude toward his twin. There had even been talk among the neighbors that Ronald's death had been a direct result of Edwin's harsh treatment. After a trivial dispute, Edwin had banished his twin from the household, and having neither money nor a place to stay, Ronald had died of pneumonia in a jail cell of a nearby town.

Mrs. Adams thought little of these accusations, however, and continued to dream on about her darling Edwin. Suddenly she turned in her chair as the smooth pattern of her thought was interrupted by a strange noise behind her. A mysterious electricity surged through her body as her eyes met those of a sleek, black cat.

The slender creature glided silently across the carpeted floor and climbed into Edwin's large red chair in the corner of the room. Mrs. Adams was so completely awestruck that she could hardly subdue her emotions enough to speak to Edwin — for of course she was positive that the silent creature was Edwin. She had always sincerely believed that he would someday return to her from his grave, although she had not expected him to be reincarnated in the form of a beautiful black cat.

In the weeks following Edwin's reappearance, any slight doubt in Mrs. Adams's mind concerning the cat's identity was completely dissolved. Not only did Edwin, as she naturally named her feline companion, share Mrs. Adams's bed and continually occupy the former Edwin's favorite red chair, but he also retired at ten o'clock every evening and rose at seven each morning, just as Edwin had habitually done for years. Mrs. Adams's large fern plant in the living room strongly irritated the cat, just as it had done Edwin, and the latter Edwin, like the former, intensely disliked tobacco smoke. Strangely enough, the slender cat even relished Edwin's favorite dish, macaroni and cheese.

There was no doubt that this was a glorious reincarnation, and the cat's strange appearance had extinguished all Mrs. Adams's loneliness and aching desire for her husband. She was just beginning to become accustomed to the joy of Edwin's company when her world was shattered and destroyed.

While she was busy in her kitchen one clear morning, she heard the sounds of a violent struggle in the yard. She hurried to the porch and witnessed in horror the sickening, bloody sight of Edwin slumping into motionless defeat before a slender, sleek, black cat — a cat identical to Edwin.

"Ronald!" she exclaimed in a terrified whisper, as she quickly drew her face away from the horrible sight.

65: The Dog That Came Back

The area was known as Porcupine's Back, because the scrubby growth on the hill behind it reminded everyone of a porcupine. It wasn't a bad sort of farm, but it stood somewhat isolated among the pine woods at the turn of the road. The big, ancient farmhouse was squat and square as a fortress.

James Morris, the owner of the farm, was rumored to have a lot of money buried on the place somewhere. He was the most unsociable person in the area. Once in a great while he and his Australian sheep dog — a splendid, blue-white creature that you couldn't get close to — would encounter a neighbor as they walked along the woodland trails, but otherwise he was scarcely ever seen.

Thus it was that when Morris and his dog disappeared, it was days, perhaps weeks, before their absence was even noticed. A lawyer who had some business with the recluse first sounded the alarm. There was no trace of the man or of his dog either. Morris couldn't have bought a rail or bus ticket without the clerk knowing it. And his old car was still in the garage, the tank full of gas.

There was the usual sort of investigation, including a search of the woods with bloodhounds, but nobody really cared about Morris and the whole matter was soon forgotten.

In the next twenty years the place had numerous occupants; it was the talk of the town, the way nobody could hold onto it. Then David Dalton bought the farm.

The new owner, like Morris, had a fine Australian sheep dog. Flash seemed oddly excited the moment he set foot on the farm. He ran all about sniffing, then lifted his head and let out a low howl. As soon as the door to the house was opened, he rushed in and went immediately to a storeroom in the back of the house. It was a small room with a cement floor — to keep out the dampness, the new occupants thought. There the dog set up the most piteous wailing and whining you ever heard. He ran to a spot in the corner near the window and began sniffing and scratching excitedly, as a dog will do when he smells a gopher.

Nothing they said would stop him, even though he couldn't make any headway against the cement. Soon his fur bristled and his wailings and whinings gave place to growls. Those growls were ferocious enough to raise the hair on the back of your neck — and Flash rarely growled as a rule.

Every time the dog was able to gain entrance to the storeroom, the same commotion would occur, and in fact, Flash's unusual behavior became worse and worse. Finally Mrs. Dalton persuaded her husband to dig next to

125

the window in the storeroom, just to ease their minds – and Flash's – by proving that nothing was there.

Dalton began to dig up the storeroom that very evening. For most of the night he dug. Breaking through the cement was no easy chore. After a while he began to feel like a fool, because he had found nothing at all. He was almost ready to give up when Flash broke into the room and started to do some digging of his own. Dalton was about to stop the dog when Flash made his first find – a cigarette lighter with the initials R. E. N.

As Dalton was turning the lighter over in his hands, his wife gave a stifled cry. Flash had uncovered a bone – not a human bone, but the skull of an animal. The skull was a large one, about the size of Flash's head. Beneath this skull, which had a hole blasted through its base, was the real find—a human skull. It too was pierced by a bullet. The skeleton followed.

The police wasted no time in identifying the skeleton. The fillings and bridgework corresponded exactly with what old Doc Batlow had put in for James Morris years before; the doctor had the yellowed records to prove it. Now it was evident that old Morris had been murdered.

The initials on the cigarette lighter seemed to belong to only one local person – Richard E. Newdick, a mason and stonecutter in the next town. He had the reputation of being a hard, cruel man, and the people of the community remembered something about his coming into a large sum of money, presumably inherited from an aunt.

Newdick was arrested by the local authorities, but the crime couldn't be proved without more evidence than the cigarette lighter. The men hit upon the idea of taking him back to the scene of the crime. Perhaps that would startle him into confessing the truth.

The day they brought Newdick to Porcupine's Back would be long remembered. Flash was sleeping in the sun. Suddenly he leaped up, as animals will often do when an enemy is scented. His fur bristled. His lips opened in a snarl, revealing the white, glistening teeth. Savage growls came from his throat. His eyes gleamed with a wolflike fierceness. Then he made a frenzied dash for the people getting out of the car. In the confusion of yells and barking one of the policemen was able to get a grip on Flash's collar. The dog would not give up; still he lunged at Newdick. Had the officer not been able to hold him, he would have torn the man's throat out then and there.

Newdick's appearance became convulsed like that of a man who has seen a ghost. His face turned white. "He's come back! Come back! Come back to get me!" Then the men realized that Flash and Morris's dog were very similar in appearance. Newdick began to rave with fear. "That's him. I've seen him in my nightmares – always knew he'd come back to get me. I've seen those burning, flashing eyes, glaring at me like they wanted to eat me up, and by the hell, I knew they would sometime, too."

Then he realized what he had said. "Yes, I killed Morris – and the dog too. I just wanted old Morris's money. I knew he had a pile hid out here somewhere. The stupid old man jumped me before I could get away, and in the scuffle I shot him through the head. I was just rising to my feet afterwards, when I saw a living thunderbolt coming towards me. There wasn't any time to think. It was the dog's life or mine. As he fell, shot in the head, with the most pitiful moaning you ever heard, I seemed to see a look in his eyes that said, 'You haven't seen the last of me.' "

The men sat staring for a moment. Each knew what the others were thinking. Perhaps Flash was Morris's dog reborn — reborn in order to catch the thief and murderer. Flash looked as if he understood what was going on. From that day on, Dalton reported, Flash would often get a look of delight in his eyes and jump up and lick the hand of someone who was not there.

Newdick was sentenced to the electric chair. Dalton and Flash got along fine, but Dalton knew that Flash belonged to someone else, someone who had gone. And that is why he is often known as the dog that came back.

66: Eloise

My grandmother told me that her sister Kate had a cat named Eloise that had lived with her for about ten years and was becoming rather set in her ways. She was accustomed to irregular happenings in the household, and they no longer upset her. She was even learning when to keep out from underfoot. She never struck my grandmother's sister as being particularly clever or attached to her. Eloise was just neutral and content.

But after Aunt Kate died, Eloise began to act strangely. Every evening after dinner she'd curl up and cry until my grandmother gave her milk with sugar in it. Aunt Kate had drunk sweetened milk with the chill taken out of it, and eventually my grandmother caught on that Eloise's whimpering was a signal that she wanted her milk warmed too. At mealtime Eloise would settle herself exactly under Kate's old place at the table. To my grandmother it seemed that the cat's behavior was growing more and more like her former mistress's. Eloise even began to crawl into bed with Uncle Harry at night, and since he was never too fond of cats, this new trick of hers didn't appeal to him in the least. He noticed, too, that she was making a nuisance of herself, and that when my grandmother spoke of the similarity of many of poor Kate's actions with those in which Eloise was now indulging, she was right.

My mother and father said my grandmother was imagining things when she pointed out the unusual habits Eloise was acquiring. They even implied that my grandmother was the one who was possessed — with the obsession of making note of a cat's ways — and that she ought to stop such nonsense.

But it surely did set my grandmother to thinking when Eloise began to take a regular walk between two and four each afternoon (for this was Aunt Kate's stroll time) and after that enjoy a snooze until dinner. Eloise even gave up running with the other cats on our street and spent the rest of her time washing and primping.

The day we bought a dog, we were really shocked into worrying about who or what was inhabiting Eloise. We had wanted a large dog for a long time, but Aunt Kate had always threatened that she'd move out if we bought one — and that she would kill it too. Well, Eloise must have housed Aunt Kate's spirit, because she ran off the day we bought a dog, never to return. And the next day, we found the dog dead.

67: Forewarned

Several years ago in Taylor County, there lived an elderly couple. One night as they slept, the woman was suddenly awakened by a noise in the room. When she sat up in bed she noticed a strange, white figure at her husband's closet. The figure appeared to be searching for something. Finally it disappeared out the door and down the steps.

The next morning the woman told her husband of this strange happening. He consoled her, as she appeared to be quite upset, and assured her that she had had a bad dream and that everything would be all right. After a while she began to believe he was right and soon forgot her supposed dream.

A few nights later she was again awakened by a strange noise. This time the figure was searching through drawers. The woman was so frightened that she screamed loudly. Awakening her husband, she was again consoled by him and reassured that it was only a dream.

The next morning the old man decided to get up early and make the journey into town to seek a doctor for his wife, since he felt she was on the verge of a nervous breakdown. While he was gone, a long black coach drawn by four black horses pulled up outside their small cottage. The man in charge, who turned out to be the mortician, came to the door seeking the body of the husband.

He told the woman that he had found her husband's clothes and personal belongings in a sack at his office that morning with a note that he had died. The note went on to tell just how he was to be dressed and put in the coffin. The body was to be picked up at the home.

Suddenly they heard a horse making a strange noise in the barn near the house. The woman was still exclaiming that the mortician had made an error as she hurried to see what all the commotion was about.

There inside the door of the barn lay her husband's dead body. The horse was their own. The husband had died in the barn even before getting started on his trip to the doctor.

The clothes the undertaker had found in his office proved to be those of her husband, and he was buried in them.

68: A Forecasted Death

Charley Hardesty and his wife had made a habit of stopping by my grandparents' house for coffee and gossip after church. One afternoon Charley told grandfather that some strange things had been happening to him all week and that he knew he was going to die very soon.

Grandfather asked him if he were ill, or what made him think that he was about to die. Charley said that he had never felt better (and indeed, he looked to be in the best of health) but while he was working in the fields or doing chores around the house, he could hear a voice calling his name and saying, "Come with me." Grandfather said it gave him a chill when Charley, in a calm, matter-of-fact way, said that he would be going with the voice before too long.

The next Sunday, Mrs. Hardesty told grandmother that something strange was going on around their farm. Charley didn't have much livestock, and the animals he had were just like pets. Down to the last chicken he had given each a name, and the animals often followed him and his wife around the farm. There was no fence around their house, but the animals seemed to know this was "sacred ground" and, with the exception of a few bold chickens, rarely came into the yard.

But this week the animals couldn't seem to get close enough to Charley. They crowded into the yard, they followed him around, pushing each other in order to get closer to him, and stranger yet, they stood around the house at night – not making a sound, but just standing there as if they were waiting for something. And the other night the horse had come all the way down from the upper pasture and pushed his nose right into the bedroom window. The banging shutter had awakened Mrs. Hardesty, although the horse himself hadn't made any noise. He just stood there staring at Charley.

"I declare, Bertha," she told grandmother, "it's just plain spooky the way those animals are acting, so quiet and all." My grandmother knew what Charley had told grandfather, but she kept quiet, knowing that if Charley had wanted his wife to know, he would have told her himself.

"And Charley," Mrs. Hardesty went on, "now *he's* the biggest mystery of all. I have been nagging at him for years to fix that leaky roof, and my garden fence, but here in this last week he must have thought I meant my threat of no more food till they were fixed. And he's told me about all the things that need to be done this winter, and who would be the best buyer for our products later in the summer."

On Wednesday morning, grandfather had just finished his chores and was leaving for the fields. Grandmother was starting to the house with the eggs when they both looked up and saw Mrs. Hardesty driving the team and wagon across the little bridge at breakneck speed. They both knew at once what must be the matter.

After the first flood of tears, Mrs. Hardesty calmed down and told them what had happened. Charley had taken longer than usual to eat his breakfast that morning, and before leaving to do his chores he had told her to keep well and safe and had kissed her forehead. Addressing an "I'm ready now" to seemingly no one, he had gone.

She had been waiting for him to bring the cream so she could make butter and noted that it was taking Charley an unusually long time to finish the milking. Glancing out the window, she saw all the animals grouped around the barn door, strangely quiet. Even the chickens had stopped their squabbling and were standing motionless.

Mrs. Hardesty said that some strange fear gripped her as she walked to the barn. Then she saw Charley. He was lying on the floor, just as he had slipped from the milking stool. The cow was standing motionless and stiff, half leaning against the opposite wall. Charley had a slight peaceful smile on his face and she knew somehow that he was dead.

The animals still acted strangely, standing forlornly about until after the funeral services were over. And the cow had to be milked outside after that, refusing to go into the stall where her master had died.

My grandparents still wonder about it. How did the animals know what was happening? And what were the strange voices Charley had heard?

69: The Fortune-Teller's Prophecy

A young man and his wife who had come to West Virginia from Italy were expecting their first child, and as was the custom in the old country, they consulted a fortune-teller about the sex and future of their child. The Italians believed that Gypsy women possessed the powers of black magic, so it was with awe and fear that the young couple approached the fortune-teller's hut.

After they had "crossed her palm with silver," the woman told them that they would have a son. But she soon dispelled their joy with the announcement that their son would be born with a knife in his hand, and that he would slay his parents. Frightened out of their wits, they hurried away.

But as the months went by, they began to look forward to the coming of their first child, and not even the Gypsy's warning disturbed them. In due time their son was born with a strange pointed object clasped in his little fist. The prophecy rushed back into their minds. Although it nearly broke their hearts, they gave the child to the young wife's cousin, who was moving to another state to find work. The boy was raised as the cousin's son, and it was only after he married and brought his beautiful wife back to the mining country of West Virginia that he was told who his real parents were.

Wanting to surprise her husband, the young wife sent a letter to his parents, asking them to come and visit. Now very old, they walked forty miles to the little mining community where their son lived. Their daughter-in-law greeted them, and since they were very tired, she gave them her bed to rest up in while she went to tell her husband, who was at work.

The foreman had let the men off early that day, and the young man approached his home a few minutes after his wife had left. Looking into the small darkened room, he saw two figures in the bed. Thinking his wife had a lover, he stepped noiselessly into the kitchen and back into the bedroom with a butcher knife.

When his wife came back she found him sitting on the edge of the bed with the knife, looking with grief and bewilderment into the faces of the parents he never knew. Thus the fortune-teller's prophecy was fulfilled.

70: The Warning Light

On August 12, 1919, something happened to me that I have never forgotten and never will forget as long as I live.

I had been dating a good-looking young man who lived in the community. The only way I was able to see him at first was to sneak out behind my mother's back, because

135

she objected to this young man. She told me that he was not a good man and would bring much sorrow to my life, but I did not listen. I went on seeing him in secret places, without her knowing it.

My mother died the next year and was buried in the small country church cemetery in our community.

After two years I was still dating the same young man. About three months before we were to be married, we had just started home from a church festival in our buggy. About three hundred yards from the church — just below the cemetery where my mother was buried — the horses began to shy and prance and rear up in the air. My boyfriend jumped out of the buggy, grabbed the horses by the bits, and held them until I could get out of the buggy. Just as I got out, the horses jerked out of his hands and ran down the road as if the devil himself were in them. There we stood with no way to get home but to walk.

As we started down the road, I saw a light in the cemetery about the size of a bushel basket. It was not a bright light — just a dim glow. It was about three feet above the ground and was moving slowly through the cemetery. It stopped and moved down into the ground, disappearing in front of my mother's grave, which was about twenty feet in front of us. I was so frightened that I began crying and shaking. It was all I could do to make it home. When we finally reached my house, I told my boyfriend good night and went inside.

I stayed in the house for about a week, trying to figure out what had happened. I finally came to the conclusion that the glow was a warning from my mother for me to break off with this young man, and that is what I did. I never again had any acquaintance with him.

Later on, my long-forgotten boyfriend married another woman, and they lived together for four years. He began to drink heavily and when he was drunk, he would beat his wife. One morning his wife's body was found. She had been stabbed to death, and her husband had disappeared.

71: Vision in the Snow

One day in the 1930s my father hailed the cab driven by his friend Karl. The big robust man with the heavy crop of reddish brown hair was strangely silent. Gone was the smile that usually spread from ear to ear. In the depths of the Depression, the cab company had put him on probation for picking up passengers who could not afford to pay their fares.

One cold December night not long after this, the office received a call for a cab to be sent to Cross Roads. The company sent Karl, but when he arrived at the designated address, there was no one living in the house. The neighbors told him that it had been vacant for several years. Thinking that some child had played a trick on the cab company, Karl started back to town.

He had driven about a quarter of a mile when he saw a beautiful, black-haired young girl standing in the middle of the road, waving for him to stop. She was oddly dressed for late December; she wore no coat, and her long, sheer, white organdy dress made ripples about her legs as the cold wintry wind blew it close to her body.

When Karl stopped to inquire if anything was wrong,

the girl asked if he would give her a ride into town. He was very reluctant to do this, since he knew he might lose his job; nevertheless, he could not bear to leave her standing by the road on such a cold night. During the ride into town, conversation flowed freely. He learned that her name was Karen. She had been to a birthday party and was in a hurry to get home in case her family might be worried. Karl thought that perhaps in her haste she had left her coat at her friend's home.

When they reached their destination, Karl turned to open the door – but the girl was gone. Concerned, he went to the house and asked Karen's parents if she had entered the house. They replied that their daughter had been dead for fifteen years. She had been killed in an automobile accident while returning home from a birthday party at Cross Roads. They explained that many people had seen her on the road, as he had. According to reports, their daughter always tried to return home on her birthday and at Christmas.

When Karl arrived at the office, there was a message for him from Karen, thanking him for his kindness. He was promptly relieved of his position with the cab company – for not charging the passenger fare.

Depressed and dejected, he left the office and walked up the street. When he met my father, he told him the story. In spite of his concern over being jobless, the old contagious smile flashed across his face as he asked, "How can you charge a ghost cab fare?"

72: The Sweater

World War I was just over and celebrations were being held by almost every town in the United States. In Shinnston the postwar celebration consisted of a big dance. My Uncle Joe had just returned from Europe and was in great spirits. He attended the dance with a few friends and neighbors.

While he was standing in the hall watching the others dance, he noticed a very beautiful young lady standing by herself. He had never seen her before, but he walked up and asked her for the next dance. She accepted, and as they danced, he found that her name was Jane McQueen. They danced the entire evening together. It was love at first sight for Uncle Joe.

When the dance was over, he walked her home. Jane's house was about six blocks from the dance hall, and, since it was getting a little chilly, Uncle Joe offered the girl his sweater. She put it over her shoulders and they walked on. When they arrived, he kissed her goodnight and she stepped inside.

Uncle Joe walked back down the street and thought of his pleasant evening. Then he remembered that Jane still had his sweater, and he decided to go back for it.

When he arrived at Jane's house again, he knocked on the door and a man answered. Uncle Joe told him he had come for the sweater Jane wore home.

The man seemed to be surprised and shocked. Tears came to his eyes. "There's some mistake. It *couldn't* have been my daughter. How can you be so foolish and cruel as to come to me on this night? My daughter died on

140

her birthday, a year ago tonight. She's buried only a few blocks from here."

Stunned beyond words, Uncle Joe turned from the tearful man and proceeded to the graveyard. When he arrived he found his sweater lying on Jane's grave.

73: The Breviary

Late one rainy evening, while driving home from a visit with a parishioner, the good Father Ireland came upon two old ladies walking along a lonely roadside. He took pity upon the two poor souls and offered them a lift. The ladies gratefully accepted the ride, directing him to a large Victorian house several miles down the road.

When the small party arrived, the two women invited the priest to share some hot tea and cake before he continued home. The evening was so cold and dismal that Father Ireland welcomed the invitation. The living room, with its old-fashioned furnishings, was comfortable though dowdy, and the fire in the old open hearth soon made it warm and cozy. Warmed by tea and pleasant conversation, Father Ireland was finally reminded by the fire's dying embers that it was very late. He thanked his hostesses and continued his way home. More than half-way to his destination, he remembered he had left his breviary on the table.

The next day Father Ireland drove back to pick it up — and found the house boarded up as if it had not been occupied for many years. It was unquestionably the same house, since it was the only one around for miles. After a thorough investigation he visited the local real estate agent and inquired about the two old ladies.

Instead of protesting, the agent assumed an air of "this has happened before," and drove with Father Ireland to the residence. After they pulled the boards away from the door and brushed cobwebs from the entrance, the old keys were fitted in the rusty lock. The door creaked open. A few steps away lay the forgotten breviary, next to some scattered cake crumbs on the table as mute testimony of the previous night's visit. Father Ireland turned to the agent amazed and asked what he knew about his friends.

After a moment's hesitation, the agent explained that the house formerly belonged to two sisters, both old maids, who for many years had invited strangers into their home for tea and respite from traveling. Frequently the two were seen walking down the road and travelers offered them a lift. They always reciprocated the kindness with hospitality. After they died, the house remained vacant. No one seemed to want the home that once had served as a welcome haven to strangers.

Months later, one of the local residents reported that he had given a ride to the same two ladies and had been entertained by them. No one paid much attention to the story at first, until gradually other people claimed they too had shared the same experience. Then the rumor grew that the old ladies had returned to continue the tradition after they had died. The spinsters had loved the old house, and it was assumed that they could not bear to leave it.

74: The Plaid Blanket

In the early 1960s a young man named Francis was driving along a lonely highway outside Paris, France, one evening at about ten o'clock. Although the highway was deserted, a very hard rain made it difficult for him to drive. As he crept along, he saw a beautiful young girl in a long white evening gown standing by the side of the road. Since she was not carrying an umbrella and he felt sorry for her, he pulled off the road and opened the door.

The girl got in and told him her name was Julie Jouvet. She gave him the address of her grandfather, with whom she lived.

Julie was trembling from the cold rain, so Francis offered her a plaid blanket, given to him by his deceased brother, to put around her shoulders. He noticed that the girl was very pale. Her skin had even a bluish cast. The couple engaged freely in conversation until they arrived at the girl's house.

Upon their arrival, Julie quickly opened the car door and ran into the house without saying goodbye, thanking him, or returning his blanket. Francis, thinking her a rather strange young woman, drove off, hoping to return the next day for his treasured blanket.

Early the following morning he drove to the girl's home, walked up on the porch, and knocked at the door. Several minutes passed before his knock was answered. Finally an old man came to the door and asked what he wanted. Francis explained that he wanted to see Julie Jouvet. The old man invited him in and introduced himself as Julie's grandfather. He was deeply interested in

143

Francis's visit. Francis explained that he had driven Julie home the night before, and she had forgotten to return the plaid blanket she had used to keep warm. He told her grandfather that if it had been just an ordinary blanket, he wouldn't have come after it, but this blanket had a special meaning. It had been given to him by his brother, who was killed in World War II, and it was the only thing he had to remember him by.

M. Jouvet told him that his granddaughter had been dead for ten years. She was killed in an automobile accident when she was eighteen years old. He said that several other young men had come to him with similar stories.

Francis could not believe what he was hearing, so he described Julie to the old man, who said his granddaughter fit the description perfectly. Francis did not believe Julie was dead and kept insisting that M. Jouvet was mistaken.

To prove himself correct, the man asked Francis to drive him to the graveyard on the outskirts of Paris, and he would show him Julie's grave and picture on her tombstone. As they drew close to the girl's grave, both men saw the plaid blanket folded neatly upon it.

75: The Lost Couple

In the late 1920s a girl and her boyfriend were on their way home from a date. As they drove along the narrow old road in the pouring rain, the wheels hit a rut and the car fell over the steep bank below. Both families were worried when the young people didn't get home that night, but they thought that perhaps the two had run away to get married, as they had so often spoken of doing.

Several weeks went by and still there was no word. Every rainy night it was reported that as people drove along the road where the couple had last been seen, the figure of a young woman in white suddenly appeared in front of the headlights, waving frantically for them to stop, but when they investigated, she would vanish.

Then one night a coal miner was on his way home from work, and when the girl appeared, he searched the heavily foliaged bank, and there were the remains of the lost car — with the couple inside, dead all that time. After that the figure was never seen again on the lonely road.

76: The Living Corpse

A young man riding home on horseback was delayed so that he had to travel at night. On his way he had to pass a cemetery. Since he was traveling by himself, he was somewhat uneasy and frightened.

All at once he came upon a young woman sitting beside the road crying. He stopped and asked if he could help. She told him that she had been walking all night, trying to get to town. She was so tired and weak that she could not go on.

He told her he would be glad to help her. He lifted her up on the black stallion, and they galloped toward town. Steadying the woman on the horse with one hand and holding the reins with the other, the man soon became tired, as the woman seemed to get heavier and heavier.

When they arrived in the town, he got off the horse to help the young woman down — and realized that she was a corpse.

The townspeople at the inn told him that every year on the anniversary of her death this woman rose from her grave, and her family then reburied her.

77: The Unhappy Bride

One night a group of boys were riding around in a car when they saw a lady in a white gown standing at an intersection. She motioned for them to stop, and when they did so she got into the car. They spoke to her, but she didn't answer. As they came near a cemetery, she motioned for them to stop. Since it was raining they were going slowly, and she jumped out of the car while it was still moving.

The boys were amazed, because they didn't see any homes near the cemetery. They went on down the road to a gas station and told the attendant what had happened. He told them a strange story.

Five years before, on that same date, a very prominent young couple from that area had been married. As they were about to leave on their honeymoon, a long line of cars was following them. They were all honking their horns and not paying too much attention to the intersection they were approaching when a large truck hit the bridal car. The groom was killed instantly and the bride died later. The legend was that the bride came back every year to wait for her husband to pick her up. The boys didn't believe the story and went back for another look.

As they approached the intersection they saw the lady once more. Again she got into the car, and again she would not speak. They asked who she was but she would not answer. When they reached the cemetery, she wanted to get out, but they wouldn't let her open the door. They turned on the inside light to see her and were startled. Her once-beautiful face was decayed. Her eyes were merely sockets in her head. As she parted her lips, she screamed and disappeared.

78: The Vanishing Lady in Black

Alex Jennings worked as a chauffeur for the wealthy Mrs. James P. Leonard in Detroit, Michigan. On this special occasion, he was working late. Mrs. Leonard was attending a dinner at the Masonic Temple and Alex decided he would go to a little restaurant a few blocks away to eat and while away the time until he should return for his employer. Finding a parking place had always been a problem around the popular little restaurant, and Alex was forced to park the car quite a distance away, but he decided the delicious food was worth the extra steps.

The parking space he found was on a small, desolate street with three old houses on each side. As he was driving along the little street, he was startled to see a lady in a black dress walking along the street to the right of his car. As surprising as her costume was the suddenness of her appearance; it was as if she had come from out of the air.

As Alex parked the car just ahead of where the lady was walking, he glanced in the mirror and saw her face staring back at him. This gave him cold chills, for her face was milk-white and her eyes were like burning coals.

Alex slowly got out and locked the car. When he

149

looked up, he saw that the lady was walking up the path to one of the houses, although it appeared to be vacant. About halfway up the walk, she turned around and looked at him again.

For some unexplainable reason, Alex decided to follow her. As he started up the walk, he glanced up – and she was gone. He was positive she had not opened the door or entered the house. He walked on up to the house, and although there were no lights on, he felt he should knock and did so, again and again, but no one answered. While he was standing there he thought he saw two eyes peer from behind a blind in the window next to the door. He finally gave up and walked on to the restaurant.

While he was eating, he kept thinking about the strange lady in black. When he returned to the car, he was still wondering what had happened to her, but it was time to pick up his employer and so he drove away.

The next day his mind kept wandering back to the lady he had seen the night before. Because everything about her was so mysterious, he decided to return to the lonely street and investigate.

When Alex arrived there, he saw an old man taking care of the lawn of the house next to the one where the strange lady had disappeared. He walked over and asked if anyone occupied the next house. The old man looked up from his work and slowly shook his head. "Not for many, many years," he replied.

"Well, that is strange," Alex said, and related the events of the previous evening.

After hearing the story, the old man had a puzzled look on his face. He decided to accompany Alex, and together they could investigate the matter. They went up the walk the lady in black had traveled the night before.

150

The porch of the house was thickly coated with dust, and Alex could see two small, dainty footprints going up the steps. The tracks reached the middle of the porch and stopped. They did not go any further or retrace. The door of the house was still about six feet from the last footprint.

Alex was more confused now than ever and asked the old man if he could explain the mystery lady. The man said that an old lady named Mrs. Ethel Jackson had lived in the house many years before. One night as she was returning from visiting her husband's grave, she collapsed on the porch of the house. She presumably died of a heart attack. As her heart was failing her, she struggled to reach the doorway, but she never made it that far. Her body was found with her hand outstretched, as if reaching for the doorknob.

79: The Phantom Lady

The only person I have ever known who has taken a ghost for a ride is my great-uncle. He used to travel around the neighboring counties, doing upholstering for various people. His two sons usually accompanied him on his longer trips. Most of these trips were dull, but one was quite extraordinary.

On this particular night there was a heavy thunderstorm. My uncle and his sons stopped at the railway station in a little town called Vienna to get something to eat. When they started out again the storm was worse than ever, for the wind had picked up, driving the rain down even harder.

They were about eight miles from the little town and were about to turn off on another road when something caught their eye. Out in the middle of the storm stood a lady in a long blue evening gown. Behind her was a cemetery. My great-uncle, quite surprised by the sight, drove over and offered her a ride.

She was soaked with rain and asked if he could take her to the railway station he had just left. He obligingly said he would and opened the door for her to get in the back seat. When they reached the station she got out of the car, thanking my uncle and his sons for all the trouble they had gone to. She then hurried toward the station.

Still a little puzzled by the incident, they started home again. About eight miles up the road, when they were again about to make the turn-off, there stood the same lovely lady in her long blue evening gown in front of the cemetery. They wondered how she could have gotten back so quickly and when they felt the back seat where she had sat, they found it quite dry.

They made their turn-off, and when they looked back, she was gone. My great-uncle drove that road many times, but he never had such an encounter again.

80: Hitchhiker at Follansbee

Some years ago, a few minutes before midnight, Tom Smarila was wearily driving from Follansbee, West Virginia to Paris, Pennsylvania. As he drove along, he noticed a hitchhiker wearing a black dress with a black veil and apparently crying. He stopped and asked the young woman if he could take her anywhere, and she got in.

Once she was in the car, she didn't say a word. All she did was sit in the front seat and weep. After about ten minutes of this constant crying, Tom offered her his handkerchief. She took it, and proceeded to dry her eyes and face.

Tom kept driving and right outside of Paris, his lights flashed on a medium-sized cemetery to the right. Immediately the young lady tapped on Tom's shoulder, and he stopped the car. She left him in the vicinity of the graveyard.

Tom went on to his work in Paris, and after work and some sleep, he decided to make a visit to the graveyard. He knew it would be dark when he got there, so he took a flashlight.

When he entered the graveyard he felt apprehensive about the whole situation, but began looking around the tombstones. About thirty feet ahead, his light hit something white. When he advanced and looked at the tombstone, he found his handkerchief draped across it with "Thanks" scratched on it in dirt.

He took the handkerchief and read the name on the headstone – Mary Ann Jonathan. When he looked at the dates on the tombstone, he saw that the girl had been twenty-six years old when she died.

Later, Tom went to the home of the girl's parents, where he was shown a picture of the young woman he had picked up and told that she had died of carbon monoxide poisoning.

What he wanted most, however – another glimpse of the dead girl – never came, although he drove the same road many times.

81: The Restless Soul

Years ago a teamster stopped at a farmhouse and asked to spend the night. The farmer didn't have enough room for him, but suggested his brother's house down the road. The brother had died five years ago and the house was haunted, but the teamster could stay there if he could stand it.

The teamster was tired and didn't believe in ghosts anyway, so he said, "I'll take the chance and stay."

He drove down, put the horses in the barn, and went into the house. It was clean-looking, as though someone was living there. He built a fire and relaxed for a little while. Then, being very tired, he blew out the oil lamp and went to bed.

He went to sleep immediately, but suddenly something awakened him by climbing into bed and getting behind him. Then the thing started twisting and turning. The teamster didn't know what to think. After a while he said, "If you are going to sleep with me, you will have to lie still."

A voice said, "I've been dead for five years, and I come back every night, but you are the first person who has spoken to me."

"What do you want?"

"When I died, I owed a neighbor fifteen dollars," replied the ghost. He named the man and said, "If you will promise that you will tell my brother to pay him, I'll leave and never come back."

"I'll pay him myself, if you'll leave and never come back," said the teamster.

"Now I can rest in my grave."

The teamster never heard another thing that night. The next morning he went to the brother's house and told him what had happened. The brother called the neighbor and asked him if his brother had owed him fifteen dollars and he said he had. The brother paid him that day, and the house was never haunted after that.

82: The Muddy Gown

When Maria was born, Doris was very proud to stand as her godmother. However, as she later found, her godchild was to bring her sadness, for eighteen years later Maria died in a car wreck. Doris tried not to think too much about the girl's death, but on All Souls' Night, she had a very strange dream.

She dreamed that Maria came to her and asked if she

155

had a gown she could lend her to wear to the procession to be held on All Souls' Night. The girl explained that when she had died they hadn't put any in the coffin, and now she needed one to wear. She asked Doris to get one of her gowns and place it by the living room door.

Doris awoke from her dream not knowing what to think. She felt obligated to do something, but felt strange because she knew Maria was dead. After a great deal of contemplation she decided to dismiss the whole matter and go back to sleep.

As sleep came over her, she began to dream again. This dream was also about Maria and much like the first. Again the girl asked for a gown – and she also asked Doris why she had not left one by the door as requested the first time. She explained again that she wanted to walk in the procession and begged her godmother to get a gown for her to wear.

Waking from her dream, Doris was more confused than ever. She decided to awaken her husband and tell him about the dreams.

Her husband thought she was probably just upset and told her to go back to sleep. She was finally persuaded to do this, but felt she must leave one of her gowns near the door. She did so and returned to bed.

Just before Doris awoke in the morning, she had another dream about Maria. The girl told her that she was sorry, but she had gotten the gown dirty. During the procession it had rained, and mud had been splashed on it.

As Doris got out of bed, she kept thinking about the last dream and hurried to the living room door where she had placed the gown. At first she thought it had never been touched; but as she picked it up, she felt that it

156

was wet, and then she noticed the mud on it. Strangely enough, it looked as if it had been worn in a procession during the rain.

83: The Roadside Stranger

In the early 1930s, a salesman who had a rural route through the central part of West Virginia had a strange experience. It was during the spring, when flash floods are quite prevalent.

As he was driving along in his car near Muddlety, he noticed a young woman waving to him from the side of the road. He stopped and offered her a ride. She got into the car, told him her name, and said he would have to take a detour because the bridge had been washed out just ahead. After showing him the way around the washout, she pointed out an old house where she said she lived, and he dropped her off and drove on.

Several miles down the road, he stopped at a rural store. Inside there were some men sitting around a Burnside stove and talking. It wasn't long before he was in the middle of the conversation. When he told of the experience he had just had, an elderly gentleman sitting in the corner looked up and asked, "What was her name?"

"Ida Crawford," the salesman answered. "Why?"

"Well," said the old man, "she's done it again." Then he told this story.

Many years before, a young woman was riding along in her carriage on a spring night. She was just passing over

157

that bridge when it collapsed from the raging flood waters. Her body was never recovered. Since then she had returned two different times, saving the lives of travelers along that route. The old man looked up and said, "You, sir, are the third."

The salesman was so astonished that he got up, walked to his car, and went back to the house where he had let the girl out. He found that the house looked as though it had been deserted for years. He searched the entire place over, looking for some clue to further information about the girl, but found none.

84: A Boy and His Dog

A boy and his dog had been missing for two days, and no one could find them. People searched everywhere, thinking that they were lost in the woods. They were eventually found in a very mysterious way.

One dark night as two railroad policemen were patrolling the tracks, they saw a strange dog about three hundred yards away. The dog seemed to glow in the dark. Holding their clubs in their hands, the policemen began to run toward the dog, but just before they reached the spot where he was standing, he disappeared before their eyes.

As the sun began to rise, the men hurried back to the spot to find out what had actually happened the previous night. When they got there, they found nothing on the trestle where they had seen the dog, so they searched the ground beneath it. There they found the bodies of the boy and his dog.

It was assumed that a train hit them and knocked them underneath the trestle where they lay. People still believe that the dog's ghost came back to help someone find the body of his master.

85: The Phantom Bridesmaid

Joe Elsey's best friend was being married in Glade Run, across Glade Pond from Joe's home. Joe planned to skate across the frozen lake to the wedding. Unfortunately business had delayed him, and he was compelled to make his journey at night.

Joe was in love with one of the bridesmaids in the wedding and this was one reason he was so anxious to attend. But Janet's father had lots of money, and Janet lived in a fine house and wore expensive clothing. This made it almost impossible for Joe to think of marrying her. He decided, however, to tell her that night that he loved her.

This determination grew as he sped along under the starlight. Suddenly he felt as if he were not alone. His eyelashes were frosted, and he thought it might have been an illusion, but right before him seemed to skate a tall, white lady. The mysterious figure was going very fast, and this aroused his curiosity. He started following the skater, though she was leading him from the route he had planned.

Joe suddenly found himself at his destination, even though his course had been altered. The mysterious skater had disappeared. As Joe took his skates off, he looked out over the part of the lake he had planned to travel. He could see blue waves through the choppy ice. If he had tried to skate there, he would now have been in a cold wet grave.

He made his way to his friend's house, where he expected to see preparations for a big wedding. When he knocked on the door, a sad-looking gentleman answered and told him that there was to be no wedding for a couple of days. Janet, the bridesmaid, had died of a terrible cold and flu.

Joe realized now who had saved him. He stayed at Glade Run till Janet was buried and his friends married. Finally Joe had to start home, but he waited until night to make his journey. He hoped to be met again by the white skater.

86: Friendship Never Dies

Paul Simon and David Young grew up in the same small town in northern Kansas. They were neighbors, and as children they were inseparable. Their friendship grew as they did, and since they were the same age, it was easier for them to stick together.

When they had completed high school they joined the marines on the "buddy plan" and received basic training together. Afterwards, both were sent to Vietnam. They were not placed in the same company upon their arrival, but they saw each other often.

Paul was the first of the two to enter an actual combat zone. His company was ordered to enter an area known to be crisscrossed with Viet Cong supply routes. Their assignment was to set up a concealed campsite and observe activities without engaging the enemy, if possible.

Paul's company had been out of the main camp about five days when they sent word that they were being attacked by a much larger force of North Vietnamese regulars. They reported many casualties, and requested immediate reinforcement.

David's company was the one chosen to reinforce his friend's. It took the second company nearly ten hours to reach the first. It was now dark and it promised to be a long night. The officers of the first company had been killed, as well as over half the men.

David was given the job of gathering the "dog tags" from the dead soldiers. With each corpse he approached, he was filled with dread, for Paul had not been accounted for. At the end of his task he was full of despair. Paul could not be found.

As the night wore on, the new company and what was left of the first braced themselves for another assault from the jungle. The attacks of the Viet Cong were varied and often deadly. They had possession of several marine uniforms, and when they made more than one attack they sometimes tried to fool the outer guards into thinking they were marines who were missing from the last battle. Some of these Vietnamese knew a few words of English and could speak them perfectly.

David was placed at a guard position along with another marine. They were instructed to shoot anything that wouldn't stop on command. The faint cry started just before dawn. David couldn't quite understand the words, but they seemed to be calling a corpsman. First he thought it was a trick, but then he worried about his friend Paul. Could his best friend be out there calling for help?

David made his way cautiously through the jungle until he came to a small clearing in the dense growth. There was a body lying at the foot of a small tree, partially covered with brush and clothed in a marine uniform, but it was not making any sounds. David approached the man slowly with his gun leveled. When he was close enough he recognized the face of his friend. He lost control of himself and fell beside the motionless body.

After a few moments he made up his mind to take Paul's body back with him. As he bent over his friend to pick him up, Paul's voice, barely a whisper, told him to "turn around and fire." He did so without thinking of where the order was coming from. He killed the Viet Cong soldier with one shot and turned to his buddy, whom he now believed to be alive. He made it back to his position without incident and sent his fellow guard to bring back a doctor.

After the guard left, David bent over Paul to see if there was anything he could do for him before the doctor came. His heart nearly stopped when he couldn't find Paul's pulse. His friend seemed not to be breathing at all.

When the doctor arrived he examined Paul and turned to David with a puzzled look on his face. David knew by now that his friend was dead. He told the doctor how Paul had warned him in the jungle only a few minutes earlier. The doctor gazed at David skeptically for a moment. Then he announced that Paul had been dead at least eight hours.

87: The Night of the Stranger

The night was very bad as Janet started on her way home. She had been to a party at a friend's house and had not realized how bad the weather had become. As she started to leave, Debbie called out to her and suggested that she stay all night, but Janet, realizing that her father would need the car and that her family would be worried, decided to go on.

After she started the car and turned down the lane, she realized how hazardous the road was and wondered if she should have stayed after all. To take her mind off her worries, she turned on the radio.

The radio started blasting out the rhythm of her favorite song and this soothed her nerves. All at once the music stopped and the announcer warned of road conditions. "Snow has blocked all the roads to Belington. Roads will not be open until morning." As Janet heard this she became more alarmed than ever. She made a hasty decision and started back.

As she neared the turn-off to Debbie's house, she realized that the snow was drifted too high to drive the car through. Not realizing the danger of such a course, she decided to park the car and walk the three-quarters of a mile.

Janet had walked for an hour and still didn't see the lights of her friend's house. She knew by now that she was lost, hopelessly wandering around in the forest. She was frightened, but tried to keep her head.

She began to feel the cold. Her fingers were getting numb and she was weary from walking. As she sat down by a huge maple tree she could feel the warmth of her body start to leave. She was exhausted, but she knew if she went to sleep she would never awaken. Nevertheless, she seemed to lose control of her senses and dozed off. Then all at once she stirred as the figure of a man seemed to pass her. She tried to jump up. It was a person! She was saved! She called the stranger to her.

Janet was unable to walk, and in order for the man to get her to the house he carried her. He was a man in his late fifties and had a huge beard. But there was something odd about him, she realized. He was wearing summer clothing and was still warm! When the man reached the door with Janet, he laid her down on the step and knocked.

When Debbie heard the knock and went to the door, she saw her friend lying on the steps. With some difficulty, she got her to the fire. As Janet began to get warm, she came to her senses.

She told Debbie everything that had happened and finished her story by telling of the man who had saved her life. She even told of his being dressed in summer clothes and seeming not to feel the cold.

As Debbie heard this she gasped and said that the man was her great-grandfather. He was believed to have been killed in the very woods in which Janet had seen him — seventy years before.

88: How?

Dewayne Poling drove to work every morning past a succession of landmarks – downtown Vienna, a small suspension bridge, and a graveyard. He returned at night by the same route.

One night it was fairly late when he was returning from his job at the power company, and night had already fallen. As he passed the little cemetery on the hill, he glanced over at it as usual. Suddenly a young man jumped out in front of the car and Dewayne couldn't stop in time – not until he had hit him. He hurriedly got out of the car and rushed over to the injured youth, who looked up and said, "Don't travel any further; the bridge is going to collapse."

Dewayne knew the man needed medical attention, and he went back to the power plant to call an ambulance. After he called, he returned to the scene of the accident. The young man seemed to be badly hurt, and when the ambulance arrived he was rushed to the hospital, but he was pronounced dead on arrival – still unidentified. Dewayne left his telephone number with the hospital attendants and told them to call when they found out the man's identity.

Meanwhile Dewayne called a construction company about the bridge. An inspection showed that the main suspension wire had been cut. If even one car had passed over it, the bridge would have fallen.

Feeling that the young man had saved his life, Dewayne wanted even more to find out who he was. A day had passed and the hospital officials decided to place a description of the youth in the *Parkersburg Sentinel,* hoping that someone could identify him.

That night an elderly lady came into the hospital and asked to see the body. When they showed it to her, a look of pride came over her face. The body was that of her son, Allan Shaw. The hospital officials asked her what she wanted done with the body, and she told them to put it back in the grave. He had been killed five years before in a car accident and had been buried in the cemetery near the suspension bridge.

They called Dewayne and went out to the graveyard. Allan's grave had been dug into and the body removed. The hospital officials passed it off as vandalism, but Dewayne couldn't. He knew he had been saved, but how?

89: Old Dork

Old Dork was getting old and would soon be taken out of the mines and replaced by a younger mule. Ever since the animal had been brought into the mines, Dan McKain had worked with him. Dan had grown to love Old Dork, and when the time came for the mule to be released from the mine, he gained permission to take him out to the farm where he lived. He wanted to see the poor aging mule spend the rest of his days in comfort.

After a time, the miners went on strike, and Dan got behind on his rent; his landlord told him he would have to vacate the house, strike or no strike. The landlord was a greedy old man, interested in no one but himself.

167

The night Dan was told he would have to leave, he went out to the barn and tenderly put his arm around Old Dork. With tears in his eyes, he explained to him the situation.

The next afternoon the landlord was walking toward town when he noticed a mule running toward him faster than any mule could possibly run. He recognized the mule as Old Dork. The animal chased him until he reached town, panting for breath.

He ran straight to the constable's home and promised to let Dan McKain live in the house for nothing if he would just get that mule off his back. Of course Dan would have to start paying rent again as soon as the mines went back to work.

The constable rode out to tell Dan the good news. He was shocked and astonished to find that Old Dork had died the preceding night in his sleep.

90: Dead Man's Curve

It all started at a New Year's Eve celebration. The clock had just struck twelve, and it was January 1, 1952. Like millions of others everywhere, Greg Hardy, his wife Joan, and their friends Sam and Doris were in a festive mood. They all had been drinking a little, but Greg said he would take them for a short ride anyway.

Greg began speeding, as his wife was afraid he would do. Then seemingly out of nowhere another car appeared, coming straight down the middle of the road. It seemed sure to hit Greg's car head on, but just in the nick of time

Greg cut sharply to the right and crashed down a steep embankment.

When the dust and smoke had cleared away, Greg climbed from the car, bleeding. He looked back inside and saw his wife and friends pinned in the car and hurt, but still alive. He started to walk up the hill to get help, and as he came near the top, he saw a stranger. The man said he was Joshua Barr from Paintsville, and he offered Greg a ride to the hospital. Just before Greg fainted, Barr promised to send an ambulance back for the others once he reached the hospital.

Several weeks later, after Greg had almost completely recovered from the accident, he decided he wanted to thank this Mr. Barr for saving his life and the lives of his wife and friends. So he got in his car and drove to Paintsville. There he found a place called Barr's General Store.

Greg went in and asked where Mr. Barr was. The storekeeper said he would show him. They both got in Greg's car, and the storekeeper told him to drive to the cemetery. There he showed Greg a tombstone inscribed,

"HERE LIES JOSHUA BARR, 1846-1906."

Greg could hardly believe it. But it was true. In fact, he was the third person to claim that he had seen Joshua Barr – who had been killed forty-five years before on that very curve.

91: The Doctor's Warning

Carol Ann Charles felt sure that her coughing spells were nothing more than a nervous reaction.

Her husband had died two weeks before, and although she had been feeling ill for the past several weeks, she had said nothing about it. She told herself that the cough would surely leave.

Half an hour past midnight on June 12, 1910, she awoke with a start. Someone was in the room.

Her husband, who practiced medicine for thirty years, had been an amateur parapsychologist and had told her many times there was nothing to fear from noises in the night.

With that in mind, she sat straight up in bed. Her husband was standing beside her, his stethoscope in his ears and his medical bag at his feet. There was a warm smile on his face, the smile she had known and loved for so many years. Nevertheless, she was frightened. She didn't say a word. She just sat there in the darkness until she fell asleep.

When she awoke in the morning, she was startled to find a sheet of paper on her bed. It was from her husband's prescription pad, and there was a note on it: "See Dr. Norton, State Street, Albany – urgent."

Thinking it was a memo he had scribbled to himself before he died, she threw it in the fireplace and dismissed the entire incident as a dream.

The following night she awoke at the same time, and there he was again – stethoscope, medical bag, and all. Only this time he wasn't smiling. There was an expression of fear and anxiety on his face. It was the expression he had reserved for stubborn patients.

His gentle smile came again, and he wrote something on a piece of paper, dropped it on the bed, and was gone. She turned on the light. The paper was from the prescription pad, with the same message.

The next morning she decided to go to Albany and see Dr. Norton, who was a dear friend of her late husband. She told him everything that had happened – the midnight visits, the notes, her husband's expression of concern, everything. His face whitened. He told her that he, too, had received nightly visitations from her dead husband, with an urgent appeal to give her an examination. He did so that day. She had tuberculosis.

Luckily, the disease was in its early stages, and within a few months she was cured completely.

Her husband's ghost never returned.

92: The Storm

Since her husband's death Sarah Dilger and her son Daniel had lived alone on their small farm about ten miles from Bergoo. Although they were secluded, Sarah was hesitant about moving into town because the farm had meant so much to her husband. However, a narrow escape from tragedy changed her mind.

The rivers were swollen from the torrential rains that had been pounding the earth for two days. This particular evening was chilly, and the wind was howling through the trees like a banshee. Firewood was running out, so Sarah asked Dan to bring more into the house. She warned him to be very careful. As she watched anxiously, he quickly gathered the fuel. He was trudging toward the house when a sudden gust of wind snapped a branch off a dead sycamore.

Sarah screamed, but it was too late. The branch struck Dan's head, knocking him off his feet. She dashed out of the house and swept him up, calling his name over and over but hearing no reply.

Dan's head was bleeding profusely, and his face was ashen. Sarah knew she must find help, but how? Bergoo was ten miles away, and the high water had washed the bridge out. She was frantic. She could see no solution.

There was a rap on the door. No, she must be imagining it. Who could be traveling on such a night? She heard another rap and cautiously opened the door. There stood two water-soaked strangers. One was short, chubby, and bald. The other was tall and lanky. Sarah immediately begged them to search out aid for her son. The short man, whose name was Martin Tucker, revealed that he was a doctor.

After a thorough examination, Dr. Tucker concluded that he must operate at once to save the boy's life. Sarah was reluctant, but she agreed to let him try. The doctor suggested that since she was so distraught, she should get some rest. As she lay on the bed, a number of questions kept plaguing her. Where had these men come from? Why did they seem so strange? Was Tucker really a doctor?

She finally dozed, and when she awakened, the operation was over. Dr. Tucker assured her that it was a success. Sarah blessed them and invited them to have dinner. She went into the kitchen to see what she could prepare for them, but when she returned, the two men were gone.

After the storm had passed, Sarah went into town and told her friends of her experience and of Dr. Tucker. Sheriff Jones looked at her with a puzzled expression on his face.

"I knew a Dr. Tucker," he said, "but he was killed five years ago in a train accident on a mercy journey."

93: Ghost Father to the Rescue

In the late 1800s the families around Smithfield were spread out and always kept to themselves. Of course, when there was help needed, one could count on any of his neighbors to lend a hand. Otherwise, everyone kept his business to himself.

One family that lived about a mile from their nearest neighbor never seemed to come out among other people. This was a very poor family of five. They farmed for most of their food and scraped for what few necessities they had to buy.

One day while the father was out in the fields plowing for the next season's planting, he became very ill. He had been overcome with the heat. He fell to the ground and called for help, but he was too far from anyone to make himself heard. There was nothing to do but lie back and try to rest.

At a neighbor's house the family had just sat down to their meal when they heard a noise outside. At the door stood a very old man in ragged clothing. The old man said that his son was in the fields plowing and needed help. The neighbor quickly put on his coat, saddled his horse, and started in the direction the old man had said his son lay. When he found the man on the ground, he went over, picked him up, and put him on the horse, so he could take him home.

After the man had rested for a time in his own house, he began to feel better. As the neighbor was talking things over, he said it was very lucky that the old father had been visiting and had gone with his son to the field. The sick man looked up in surprise and said, "My father! What do you mean? My father has been dead for five years."

94: A Timely Warning

A deep autumn haze hung low over the wooded area of Smokehole. The brisk wind rustled the leaves on the ground. This was the first day of the hunting season.

As the sun rose, bright and promising, the hunters were already in the woods trying to shoot their quota of squirrels for the day. The squirrels sensed the danger and did not venture out of their soft hiding places. As a result, not many hunters were successful, so they decided to try their luck the next morning.

Frank Genson and his son Bob did not return to the lodge. They decided to make camp and spend the night in the woods. This would give them the advantage of being up earlier and perhaps having better luck. A hasty meal was prepared over a fire built on a large flat rock. The sun was fading very fast and the forest took on the deep purple and dusty gray colors of evening. A peaceful quietness fell over the forest and all sounds of animal life came to a stop. The two men placed their sleeping bags near the fire to keep warm and felt secure within the circle of the red glow. In the fading twilight a hunter appeared from nowhere. A hound dog, wagging his tail, followed close at his heels. Both man and dog stood just outside the fire's glow.

"Men, I wouldn't camp here for the night," he said. He explained that underneath the flat rock was a rattlesnakes' nest. "Your fire is heating the rock now," he said, "and before morning the rattlesnakes will come out and bury their fangs in you."

He turned to go and waved a hand with a missing left forefinger. After a few steps, he and his dog vanished from sight.

A bright fire welcomed the men back at the lodge. They sat down to talk with the other hunters and told them of their visitor with the missing left forefinger — and his warning.

"Missing left forefinger?" one of them asked. "Why that's the ghost of Tom Martin. Ten years ago Tom camped on that very same rock and was found dead the next morning. His body had several fang marks of rattlesnake bites."

95: The Ghost of the Rails

A neighbor of ours tells this story of his youth. He had been a wild, headstrong young man and had wanted to see all of our beautiful country before he settled down. So at seventeen he had packed a few things, left a note for his folks, and hopped a freight train to a new, exciting life. Mr. Lantz is an old man now and his wanderlust is cured, but he says that on stormy nights he always remembers the strange events of a trip from Cleveland to his home town of Rowlesburg, West Virginia.

It was during the winter of 1919, he says, that he walked to the outskirts of Cleveland, planning to hop a freight that was going close to home. After waiting a few minutes, he was surprised to notice a man squatting on his heels by the tracks. He had not heard him walk up. He remarked on the stranger's quietness and then asked him where he was bound, for judging from his gear he was a rail bum too.

Without turning, the man told him he was going to Rowlesburg. Mr. Lantz was delighted to find he would have a companion for the trip, but his friend wasn't very encouraging when he heard that the boy intended to join him.

"No," he said, "you aren't going to be on the 11:15!"

At first, Mr. Lantz was a little angry, and then he began to laugh. He told the stranger that he'd "make it" – with more confidence than he felt.

The stranger said, "No!" again, more sharply and strangely than before.

"Why not?" Mr. Lantz asked. "And why don't you come over here by the fire where I can see you?"

The strange man just sat there, staring at the rails. Again Mr. Lantz was slightly angry and began to douse the fire. He could hear the whistle of the 11:15 in the distance. His companion got up slowly, his back to him as he was preparing to leave.

"That train will cause your death," he said in his slow chilling voice.

Mr. Lantz just stared at him, noticing for the first time that his shirt, a red and green plaid, was streaked with blood. Muttering "You're crazy!" under his breath, he bent to finish dousing the fire. He confessed that he was in a great hurry to leave, for he was afraid of the man, and angry with himself for being afraid.

Suddenly, he heard the man say, "You aren't going on that train, mister!" — right in his ear.

He turned quickly and the sight of that man's face chilled him. It was traced in patchwork fashion with still-bloody scars, and his whole face was twisted out of shape, the eyes bulging with a look of horror.

Mr. Lantz stared, speechless, and then tried to push the horrible creature out of the way — but his hand went right through him. He screamed and then fainted. When he regained his senses, the train had gone and so had his companion.

When Mr. Lantz arrived in Rowlesburg the next day, he went straight into the depot to see if Mike, the Irish janitor, would give him a handout. He ate his fill and started to go. Then he couldn't resist asking any longer.

"Mike, did a strange fellow drop off here yesterday?"

Mike answered that nobody had dropped, but someone had *tried* to jump off the Cleveland Special and had been caught beneath the wheels. No two pieces of him ended

178

up in the same place — the only thing left was a piece of plaid shirt.

"Red and green plaid?" Mr. Lantz asked, fearing the answer.

"Sure, and how did you know?"

Mr. Lantz says he thinks of it often. He had heard of ghosts coming back, but he says he never heard of one traveling forward in time.

96: The Lady in White

It was late in the afternoon, many years ago, when my grandfather and his brother were riding back from town. When they were just a few miles from the farm, they noticed another rider a little way in front of them. Since it was dusk, they could not make out who it was. All they could tell was that the person was dressed in white and was riding a white horse. They knew all the people who lived around them and all of their stock, but they did not recognize the horse or the rider.

Since it was getting dark, they decided to ride up and see if they could be of any assistance to the stranger. As they drew nearer, they recognized the rider to be a lady. This seemed very strange to them, since a woman riding the backwoods at that time of night was not a common thing.

As they approached the young woman, my great-uncle called out to her. This seemed to frighten her horse, because it began to gallop after he called. It looked as if

179

the rider couldn't control the horse, so my grandfather and his brother galloped after her.

They followed the woman over fields and onto a seldom-used road. A little way up the road they saw a buggy overturned in front of them. The lady in white rode right past the buggy – not even slowing down to see if she could offer any assistance. She then turned off and rode into the woods.

When my grandfather and his brother reached the buggy, they saw it was their mother's. It was now a wreck; it looked as if it had turned over several times, and it had landed against some rocks. They could not see their mother anywhere around.

All of a sudden the lady in white rode out from the woods a few yards down the road. My grandfather ran over to where she had been and found his mother lying there, unconscious but alive.

When they got her home and she was feeling better, she explained that she had been out visiting and decided to take a shortcut home. Something had frightened her horse, and he began to run. Then a wheel hit a hole and the buggy overturned; that was the last thing she remembered.

She asked what made the boys take this out-of-the-way road, and they explained that they had seen and followed the lady in white. They told her how they had found the buggy, but at first couldn't see its driver. Then they explained how the lady in white led them to the spot where she had been thrown out.

They never found any further sign of the lady in white or heard anything more about her. But they believed if it had not been for this mystery woman they might never have gotten their mother back alive.

NOTES

1. A Strange Illusion

Harvey Thorp, Grafton, 1965, as told to him by an old lady who lived in the Grafton area. Her grandfather was the traveler.

Motifs — V229.21: House and family appear overnight to shelter priests (variation); E230: Return from dead to inflict punishment.

2. The Jailer's Dog

Jeff Smith, 1965, as told to him by his grandfather, now of Fairmont, but formerly of Brownsville, Pennsylvania.

Motifs — E232: Return from the dead to slay wicked person; B299.1: Animal (ghost) takes revenge on man.

3. Coffin Hollow

Charles Shaver, Monongah, 1967.

Motif — E232.1: Return from dead to slay own murderer.

4. Earl Booth's Pot of Gold

Daniel O'Brien, Barbour County, 1965.

Motif — E234.3: Return from dead to avenge death.

5. Revenge of an Oil Worker

Denver Kendall, Mobley (near Smithfield), 1965, as told to him by his father.

Motifs — E234.4: Ghost an unjustly executed man; Q556: Curse as punishment.

6. The Shue Mystery

Eleanor Harper, Parsons, 1967. Evidently, this is based on an actual happening. The young wife did die, was buried, and her mother testified that her daughter appeared to her four times and told how she was murdered. The husband was convicted and hanged after the wife's body was dug up and an autopsy performed.

Motifs — E231: Return from dead to reveal murder; E231.1: Ghost tells name of murderer.

7. The Peddler's Story

Eleanor Harper, Parsons, 1967. The murder was confirmed by the wife, and no one has lived in the house since, evidently.

181

Motifs — E281: Ghost haunts house; E231.5: Ghost returns to murderer, causes him to confess (variation: here the *wife* confesses).

8. The Black Dog Ghost

John Joseph Martray, 1965, student from Connelsville, Pennsylvania, as told to him by his grandfather.

Motifs — E521.2: Ghost of dog; E230: Return from dead to inflict punishment.

9. The Barn Ghost

Harvey Thorp, Grafton, 1965, as told to him by his grandmother, who heard it from her father many times.

Motif — E232.1: Return from dead to slay own murderer.

10. The Miner's Wife

John Joseph Martray, 1965, as told to him by his grandfather.

Motif — E230: Return from dead to inflict punishment.

11. Yankee Thrift

Myra Townsend, Huntington, 1963, as told to her by her grandfather, as his own experience.

Motifs — E281: Ghosts haunt house; E293: Ghosts frighten people (deliberately); E275: Ghost haunts place of great accident or misfortune.

12. The Mysterious Music

Charles Hannum, 1969, as experienced by him and his friends.

Motifs — E530: Ghosts of objects (house); E402: Mysterious ghostlike noises heard.

13. The Last Lodge of Ravenswood

Thomas Schoffler, Ravenswood, 1970. This is his own experience.

Motif — E275: Ghost haunts place of great accident or misfortune.

14. The Farmhouse Ghost

Carol Marks, 1966, as told to her by her aunt.

Motif — E281.3: Ghost haunts particular room in house.

15. The Wealthy Widower

Linda Richards, 1966, as told to her by a dormitory student.

Motif — E236.4: Return from dead because last will was not fulfilled.

16. The Ghost of Hangman's Hollow

Richard Swick, 1963, as told to him by an older relative in Gilman — just outside of Elkins.

Motif — E334.2.2: Ghost of person killed in accident seen at death or burial spot.

17. The Haunted Field

Theresa Britton, Rowlesburg, 1966, as told to her by her grandfather.

Motif — E275: Ghost haunts place of great accident or misfortune.

18. The Misty Ghost

Theresa Britton, Rowlesburg, 1966, as told to her by her grandfather.

Motif — E275: Ghost haunts place of great accident or misfortune.

19. The Murdered Girl

Jeanette Coger.

Motif — E231.1: Girl tells name of murderer.

20. The Hitchhiking Ghost of Buttermilk Hill

Richard Stickler, Marion County, 1964, as told to him by Mrs. Luella Freeland of Monumental, as her own experience.

Motif — E272.2: Ghost rides behind rider on horse.

21. Midnight Whippoorwill

Sheila Ireland.

Motifs — E337: Ghost reenacts scene from own lifetime; E451: Ghost finds rest when certain thing happens.

22. Galloping Horses

Mrs. Florena Duling, Fairmont, 1972, as told to her by her mother, Mrs. Arna Becker Evans, many times.

Motifs — E363: Ghost returns to aid living; E321: Dead husband's friendly return.

23. A Confederate Soldier

Eleanor Harper, Parsons, 1967. Evidently this is a well-known story in Tucker County.

Motifs — E281.3: Ghost haunts (ghosts haunt) particular room in house; E279.2: Ghost disturbs sleeping persons; E337: Ghost reenacts scene from own lifetime.

24. Return from Death
Elizabeth Barnard, Elkins area, 1967.
Motifs — E327: Dead father's friendly return; E363.1: Ghost aids living in emergency.

25. A Face in the Window
Elizabeth Barnard, Elkins area, 1967.
Motifs — E281: Ghosts haunt house; E275: Ghost haunts place of great accident or misfortune.

26. A Ghostly Avenger
Alan Hawkins, 1966.
Motif — E230: Return from dead to inflict punishment.

27. Darkish Knob
Eleanor Harper, Parsons, 1967.
Motif — E275: Ghost haunts place of great accident or misfortune.

28. A Slave Boy's Revenge
Robert Nichols, Millersville, 1966.
Motif — E232.1: Return from dead to slay own murderer.

29. Frist House
Robert Fertig, Hardy County, 1966.
Motif — E275: Ghost haunts place of great accident or misfortune (ghosts here).

30. The Murdered Prisoner's Ghost
Mrs. Julia Gulas, Fairmont, 1966.
Motif — E275: Ghost haunts place of great accident or misfortune.

31. The Cole Mountain Light
Robert Fertig, Hardy County, 1966.
Motif — E530.1: Ghost-like lights (light).

32. The Crying Baby of Holly
Richard Swick of near Elkins, 1963.
Motifs — E225: Ghost of murdered child; E425.3: Revenant as child; E275: Ghost haunts place of great accident or misfortune.

33. A Strange Fire
Linda Richards, 1967, as told to her by her aunt, who was one of the two women. Andrew Muhar, Greene County, Pennsylvania, supplied a close variant of this tale.

Motifs — E225: Ghost of murdered child; E275: Ghost haunts place of great accident or misfortune.

34. Jones's Hollow
Janet Everson, Barbour County, 1964, as told to her by her grandmother.
Motif — E275: Ghost haunts place of great accident or misfortune.

35. Who Was Guilty?
Myra Townsend, Huntington, 1963, as told to her by her grandmother, who in turn learned it from her father.
Motifs — E275: Ghost haunts place of great accident or misfortune; E234.4: Ghost an unjustly executed man.

36. The Cooke Family
Janet Everson, Barbour County, 1964, as told to her by her grandmother, Mrs. J. N. Champ of Belington.
Motif — E275: Ghost haunts place of great accident or misfortune.

37. The Ghosts of the Mine Horses
Richard Stickler, Marion County, 1964, as told to him by Mr. L. C. B.
Motifs — E275.1: Ghost haunts mine after tragedy (ghosts haunt); E423.1.3: Revenant as horse(s).

38. The Ghost of Old Ben
Lois Puskas, Grant Town, 1964, as told to her by her stepfather, Mr. Martin Beckish, a miner.
Motifs — E326: Dead brother's friendly return; E336.1: Helpful mine ghosts.

39. Friends to the End
Bob Parker, Grant Town, 1964.
Motif — E336.1: Helpful mine ghosts.

40. The Invisible Friend
Dave Stuart, 1965, as told to him by his mother.
Motifs — E275.1: Ghost haunts mine after tragedy; E336.1: Helpful mine ghosts.

41. Eighty Feet Deep
Penny Stanley, 1965. One of the legends of Prickett's Fort.
Motifs — E234.3: Return from dead to avenge death (murder); E275.1: Ghost haunts mine after tragedy.

42. The Swinging Lantern
Steve Noe, 1966, who says this has never been explained.
Motifs — E275: Ghost haunts place of great accident or misfortune; E530.1: Ghost-like lights (light).

43. Van Meter's Plight
Doug Jacobs, Grant County, 1966, as told to him by Mrs. Frank Van Meter of Dorcas.
Motifs — E422.1.1: Headless revenant; E275: Ghost haunts place of great accident or misfortune.

44. The Old Man's Reward
Sammy Skeen, Ripley, 1966.
Motifs — E422.1.1: Headless revenant; E371: Return from dead to reveal hidden treasure.

45. The Headless Man
Nancy Ice, 1965.
Motifs — E265: Meeting ghost causes misfortune; E422.1.1: Headless revenant.

46. Dog Rock
Richard Stickler, 1964, as told to him by Lawrence Conaway.
Motif — E521.2.2: Headless ghost of dog.

47. The Headless Dog of Tug Fork
Sammy Skeen, Ripley, 1966.
Motifs — E521.2.2: Headless ghost of dog; E272.2: Ghost rides behind rider on horse.

48. The Legend of the Haunted House
Diana Musgrave, Clarksburg area, 1965, as told to her by her grandfather. It is one of the few legends sincerely believed by the people of this area.
Motifs — E337.1.1: Murder sounds heard just as they must have happened at time of death; E337.2: Re-enactment of tragedy seen; E275: Ghost haunts place of great accident or misfortune (ghosts haunt).

49. The Man on the Railroad
Kathleen Christy, 1967, as told to her by her grandmother, Mrs. Jack Hedmond, whose parents actually remembered the event in Colliers. The great-grandparents were Mr. and Mrs. Petrelle.
Motif — E337.2: Re-enactment of tragedy seen.

50. The Girl in the Green Coat
Nancy Ice, 1965.
Motif — E337.2: Re-enactment of tragedy seen.

51. The Blue Gown
Brenda Lilly, 1966, as told by her friend's father, Mr. Sirk, who had this experience as a boy.
Motif — E337.2: Re-enactment of tragedy seen.

52. Returning Suicide
Mrs. Gerry Vilor, Fairmont, 1968.
Motifs — E281: Ghosts haunt house; E293: Ghosts frighten people (deliberately).

53. The Old Gray Mare Conquers the Unknown
Myra Townsend, Huntington area, 1963, as told by her great-uncle.
Motif — E421.1: Invisible ghosts.

54. The Haunted House of Shell Creek
Kathy Willey, student from Cambridge, Maryland, 1966.
Motif — E275: Ghost haunts place of great accident or misfortune.

55. The Light in Mother's Room
Theresa Britton, Rowlesburg, 1966.
Motif — E419: Other restless dead (mother cannot rest when children quarrel about property).

56. The Lynchers
Harvey Thorp, Grafton, 1968.
Motifs — E234.3: Return from dead to avenge death (murder); E234.4: Ghost an unjustly executed man.

57. The Cline House
Robert Fertig, Hardy County, 1966.
Motif — E281.0.1: Ghost kills man who stays in haunted house.

58. The Seated Lady
Sheila Ireland.
Motifs — E210: Dead lover's malevolent return (variation); E273: Churchyard ghosts.

59. The Power of Love
Pat Cloan, Weston, 1966, as told to him by old J. W. Collins, the cemetery caretaker near Pat's home.

Motifs — E1: Person comes to life; E165: Resuscitation of wife by husband giving up half his remaining lifetime (variation; actually, through *love* here); E125: Resuscitation by relative (husband).

60. Death of a Minister's Wife
Pam Parrish, 1967, as told by her Great-uncle Bruce, as a family experience.
Motifs — E1: Person comes to life; E58: Resuscitation by weeping; E63: Resuscitation by prayer; E177: Resuscitated man (woman) relates visions of beyond.

61. Lamented Love
Myra Townsend, Huntington area, 1963, as told to her father by his Aunt Pearl, when he was a young boy living on a farm.
Motifs — E275: Ghost haunts place of great accident or misfortune; E631: Reincarnation as plant (tree) growing from grave.

62. The Rosebush
Harvey Thorp, Grafton, 1965, as told to him by his Aunt Georgia, who heard it when she was a girl.
Motif — E631: Reincarnation as plant (tree) growing from grave.

63. The Dead Girl Revived
Mrs. Mary McDougal, Fairmont, 1972.
Motifs — E1: Person comes to life; E127: Resuscitation by friends.

64. Twice Twins
Pat Sloan, Weston, 1966, as told to him by his Aunt Martha, who knew the widow involved. (Names have been changed.)
Motifs — E610: Reincarnation as animal; E611.5: Man reincarnated as cat.

65. The Dog That Came Back
Martha Jane Neer, 1964, as told to her by an old man in the southern part of the state.
Motifs — E658: Reincarnation: animal to another animal; E693: Reincarnation for revenge.

66. Eloise
Stanley Twarnowski, as a supposedly true family experience.
Motif — E725.1: Soul leaves man's body and enters animal's.

67. Forewarned
Harvey Thorp, Grafton, 1968, as told to him by his grandmother.

Motif – D1810.8.3.2: Dream warns of danger which will happen in near future.

68. A Forecasted Death
Theresa Britton, Rowlesburg, 1966, as told to her by her grandparents.
Motifs – D1812.0.1: Foreknowledge of hour of death (variation); B120.0.1: Animals have second sight; B141.2.1: Horse weeps for master's (saint's) approaching death (variation).

69. The Fortune-Teller's Prophecy
Theresa Britton, Rowlesburg, 1966, as told to her by her grandmother.
Motifs – D1712: Soothsayer; N323: Parricide prophecy unwittingly fulfilled.

70. The Warning Light
Richard Stickler, Marion County, 1964, as told to him by Mrs. Luella Freeland of Monumental, as her own experience.
Motif – E530.1.5: Ghost light indicates impending calamity.

71. Vision in the Snow
Myra Townsend, Huntington area, 1963, as told to her by her father.
Motif – E332.3.3.1: The Vanishing Hitchhiker.

72. The Sweater
John Marchio, Shinnston, 1967, as told to him by his uncle.
Motif – E332.3.3.1: The Vanishing Hitchhiker.

73. The Breviary
Larry Torchia, Clarksburg, 1965, as told by another priest.
Motifs – E332.3.3.1: The Vanishing Hitchhiker(s); E363: Ghost returns to aid living.

74. The Plaid Blanket
Carol Marks, 1966.
Motif – E332.3.3.1: The Vanishing Hitchhiker.

75. The Lost Couple
Mrs. Gerry Vilor, Fairmont, 1968.
Motif – E332.3.3.1: The Vanishing Hitchhiker.

76. The Living Corpse
David Shaffer, Marion County, 1965, as told to him by his grandmother.
Motif – E332.3.3.1: The Vanishing Hitchhiker.

77. The Unhappy Bride
Claudia Kopp, 1966, as told to her by a friend whose grandmother knew the boys who picked the girl up. This was supposed to have happened in the northern part of the state.
Motifs — E332.3.3.1: The Vanishing Hitchhiker; E334.2.3: Ghost of tragic lover haunts scene of tragedy.

78. The Vanishing Lady in Black
Linda Richards, 1967, as told to her by her roommate, whose uncle was Mr. Alex Jennings.
Motif — E334: Non-malevolent ghost haunts scene of former misfortune, crime, or tragedy.

79. The Phantom Lady
Kathy Willey, Cambridge, Maryland, 1966; supposedly a relative's experience.
Motif — E332.3.3.1: The Vanishing Hitchhiker.

80. Hitchhiker at Follansbee
Larry Bell, 1968, as told to him by Tom Smarila of Follansbee.
Motif — E332.3.3.1: The Vanishing Hitchhiker.

81. The Restless Soul
Sheila Ireland, 1965.
Motif — E415.4: Dead cannot rest until money debts are paid.

82. The Muddy Gown
Kathy Gettings, 1966, as told to her mother by one of her Italian friends.
Motifs — E300: Friendly return from the dead; E720.1: Souls of human beings seen in dream.

83. The Roadside Stranger
Richard Browning, 1965.
Motifs — E332.3.3.1: The Vanishing Hitchhiker; E363.3: Ghost warns the living.

84. A Boy and His Dog
Record of contributor's name lost.
Motif — E377: Return from dead to teach living (variation: to show by luminous light where the bodies are, or help locate them).

85. The Phantom Bridesmaid
Harvey Thorp, Grafton, 1964, as told to him by his grandmother, who lived her entire life in Mannington, West Virginia. She heard this at a creamery where she worked.

Motif – E363: Ghost returns to aid living.

86. **Friendship Never Dies**

Thomas Schoffler, Ravenswood, 1968, as told to him by his uncle, who spent two years in Vietnam as a marine sergeant.

Motif – E363: Ghost returns to aid living.

87. **The Night of the Stranger**

David Stuart, Philippi, 1965. Told to him by his fiancée as her own experience.

Motif – E363: Ghost returns to aid living.

88. **How?**

Larry Bell, 1968. Told to him by Mr. Dewayne Poling of Vienna in Wood County, West Virginia, as his own experience.

Motif – E363: Ghost returns to aid living.

89. **Old Dork**

Bob Parker, Grant Town, 1964.

Motif – E363: Ghost returns to aid living.

90. **Dead Man's Curve**

Bob Carpenter, 1966, as told to him by a friend from Grafton.

Motif – E363: Ghost returns to aid living.

91. **The Doctor's Warning**

Harvey Thorp, Grafton, 1966.

Motif – E363: Ghost returns to aid living.

92. **The Storm**

Linda Rogers, Webster Springs, 1965.

Motif – E363: Ghost returns to aid living.

93. **Ghost Father to the Rescue**

Denver Kendall, Smithfield area, 1965, as told to him by his father.

Motif – E363: Ghost returns to aid living.

94. **A Timely Warning**

David Cimino, Fairmont area, 1964.

Motif – E363: Ghost returns to aid living.

95. **The Ghost of the Rails**

Theresa Britton, Rowlesburg, 1966, as told by a neighbor, the Mr. Lantz of the story.

Motif – E363: Ghost returns to aid living.

96. **The Lady in White**

John Marks, 1969, as told in his family.

Motif – E363.1: Ghost aids living in emergency.

BIBLIOGRAPHY

Baughman, Ernest W. *Type and Motif-Index of the Folktales of England and North America*. Indiana University Folklore Series, no. 20. The Hague: Mouton, 1966.

Beardsley, Richard K., and Hankey, Rosalie. "A History of the Vanishing Hitchhiker." *California Folklore Quarterly* 2(1943): 13-44.

———. "The Vanishing Hitchhiker." *California Folklore Quarterly* 1(1942): 303-35.

Byrne, Patrick. *Irish Ghost Stories*. Cork: Mercier Press, 1968.

Carmer, Carl. *The Screaming Ghost and Other Stories*. New York: Knopf, 1956.

Creighton, Helen. *Bluenose Ghosts*. Toronto: Ryerson, 1957.

Harden, John. *Tar Heel Ghosts*. Chapel Hill: University of North Carolina Press, 1954.

Jones, Louis C. "Hitchhiking Ghosts in New York." *California Folklore Quarterly* 3(1944): 284-92.

———. *Spooks of the Valley*. Boston: Houghton Mifflin, 1948.

———. *Things That Go Bump in the Night*. New York: Hill and Wang, 1959.

Lowndes, Marion S. *Ghosts That Still Walk: Real Ghosts of America*. New York: Knopf, 1941.

Musick, Ruth Ann. *The Telltale Lilac Bush and Other West Virginia Ghost Tales*. Lexington: University of Kentucky Press, 1965.

Randolph, Vance. *Ozark Superstitions*. New York: Columbia University Press, 1947.

———. *The Devil's Pretty Daughter*. New York: Columbia University Press, 1955.

Reynolds, James. *Ghosts in American Houses*. New York: Bonanza, 1955.

———. *More Ghosts in Irish Houses*. New York: Farrar, Straus and Cudahy, 1956.

Seymour, St. John D., and Neligan, Harry L. *True Irish Ghost Stories*. Dublin: Hodges, Figgis, 1914.

Thompson, Stith. *Motif-Index of Folk Literature*. Enl. and rev. ed. 6 vols. Bloomington: University of Indiana Press, 1955-1958.

West Virginia Folklore. Ghost story issues: 3, no. 1 (Fall 1952); 5, no. 1 (Fall 1954); 7, no. 1 (Fall 1956); 9, no. 1 (Fall 1958); 10, no. 1 (Fall 1959); 13, no. 1 (Fall 1962); 14, no. 1 (Fall 1963); 15, nos. 1 and 2 (Fall and Winter 1964).